SOSI

# SOSI

Linda Ghan

*Signature*
EDITIONS

Cover design by Terry Gallagher/Doowah Design.
Photo of Linda Ghan by Toby Gilsig.
Cover rug courtesy of Janice Summers.
Printed and bound in Canada by Marquis Book Printing.

Acknowledgements
There are many people in many locations who have contributed in story, in fact, and in encouragement. First, I must thank Kerop Bedoukian, whose zest for life inspired this book. Kerop single-handedly sponsored 2000 Armenian families to Canada from Turkey in the 1950s and, it should be mentioned, could read oriental carpets as others read fingerprints. Thanks also to Vartuhi Yegyayan Kermoyan, who shared the painful memories of leaving Turkey in the same period, to Sossi Galentz, whose passion for her subject was important in informing this book. I thank Harold Bedoukian, who was ever ready for yet another question: I spent many afternoons at Ararat Rugs surrounded by carpets and going through books. I thank Cornerstones in London, England for editorial advice, as well as Jenny Raynor and Jonathan Pegg. Others unfailingly patient were: Leslie Bellamy, Haruyo Kobayashi, Donna Langer, Bill Landry, Claire Helman, Sheila Arnopoulous, and Sheila Fischman.

We acknowledge the support of The Canada Council for the Arts and the Manitoba Arts Council for our publishing program.

Library and Archives Canada Cataloguing in Publication

Ghan, Linda
    Sosi / Linda Ghan.

ISBN 1-897109-06-7

    1. Armenian massacres, 1915-1923 -- Fiction.  I. Title.

PS8563.H36S68 2005          C813'.54          C2005-906449-8

Signature Editions
P.O. Box 206, RPO Corydon, Winnipeg, Manitoba, R3M 3S7

In memory of
Kerop Bedoukian,
a survivor, a humanitarian, a storyteller.

# PROLOGUE

I was born on the high plains of Turkey where the air is so fine and clear, it is as though you see across space into dream. The open plateau, ringed in the distance by the peaks of rose granite mountains, was filled with crystal light, and we did our best, painting shutters and doors blue, to entrap it. Blue was the colour of protection. Of strength. I had blue eyes. Mama had blue eyes. We were the wonder of the village — if a cat's-eye, a polished stone which was the mere resemblance of an eye, could ward off evil, what power was there in us with our living blue? As if that wasn't enough, I was named for the prophet Mohammed's daughter. Zeyneb. Blessed one. With a name like that, with my blue eyes, what could I not escape at my own choosing?

I had another name as well, an Armenian name, the one Mama had given me, Sosi Arta. This was a secret name which afforded no protection. Each new year — not the Muslim New Year, but our own, the Armenian New Year — Mama and I wound a thread around our wrists, a thread blood-red, a thread of life with many tiny knots, each knot a prayer. Each new year she hung a new cross at my neck. She made it out of bread dough. In time of danger, one could eat such a cross.

Our knotted prayer threads my father did not mind, but at the sight of the cross, his eyes would blaze: surely my mother of all people should understand. My mother would say nothing then, as loneliness crept into her eyes and helplessness into his.

During the winter days, long in their seclusion, Mama wove in the colours of darkness, blood red and blackest blue, graceful birds taking shape to dance life across the plains and valleys of her carpet. These, the valleys which hid the rose and pomegranate courtyard of her youth, my mother no longer believed existed, for Allah had taken them, as surely as he had taken her from them.

My mother blamed Allah, and my grandfather, though born into Islam and holding still to many Muslim tenets, did not correct her. Allah, she believed, was a god of vengeance, and Jesus had been a god of kindness. Jesus was a gentle memory to whom she prayed.

My grandfather roared at Allah, roared at any sort of god, but he allowed her the prophet Jesus. Who needed Allah in the mountains anyway? Allah was for the town sheep who had neither the stars in their hair, nor the mountain tapestry at their feet. Since Allah had failed him, all gods, all prophets were in contempt: it was in the name of Allah that the infidels, men like him who cried for their sheep and bled for their children, were struck down. Vineyards and fields, kitchens and courtyards, still filled with the laughter and tears of those who had been wrested from them, was the reward of those who murdered in the name of Allah. He had fled, a Turkish soldier plucking life, a blue-eyed child, out of the maelstrom. He promised her mother, who at first misunderstood his intentions and fought him under the burning sun with a fierce dying strength, that he would allow the child her memories and her truth.

My grandfather loved her with a passion born out of that violent sun. And she loved him violently in return. He and only he of the entire village knew that he had saved an Armenian child who, though she soon spoke Turkish and learned the ways of Islam and of prayer, nevertheless, while bowing to Mecca, remained Armenian in her heart and soul. Yet she had only the simple prayers and stories and the elegant bird-letter alphabet that she had been taught by an older sister, letters she drew over and over again in the snow or in the red mountain earth. She grew and learned to trust one other, a child her age: they were betrothed.

I was five when the fierce, laughing, loving part of my grandfather disappeared one day, and he lay stiff on the floor. "Dead," my mother said. "Gone to Jesus." She laughed a bitter laugh. I do not think she cried. I do not think she ever cried. She mourned his death with a dry and bitter pain.

That spring, my sixth (an assurance, my mother said, that I would live to comfort her in her old age as four others before me had not) I brought her bits of filigree ice crusts carved out by the spring sun, news of the first shy warbler. But her bitterness remained.

My mother had no friends in the village. During the harvest the other women worked together swinging their small hand scythes in rhythm with their chatter, but my mother never lifted her eyes nor left my father's side. Yet I had many friends. One child was treated like another, given a kiss or cuff as required. I was my mother's blue-eyed child, but I belonged to them, too.

I questioned neither Allah nor Jesus: they were in the sky, each in his separate courtyard. I never doubted that I would grow, as my mother had, to be a woman and to give life. I never doubted that I would be with my mother always.

One day when I was out with the other children tending the long-haired goats, a kid, less certain than the others, slipped, and trembled, trapped between the steep bank and the rushing spring river. Running to its aid, I made the sign of the cross.

"Infidel!"

I stopped. The single cry of surprise was taken up to become jeers, taunts — a threat. I bent to pick up the kid. A rock struck my back. I scrambled up the bank, down the long slope to our village, through the white-walled streets, into the safety of our courtyard. "Infidel! Infidel!" Mama ran to our gate, screaming a curse at my pursuers that she swore even Allah would never undo. She knelt, clasped the two of us, child and kid, and moaned her guilt: "God did not want me to live."

We slipped out of our courtyard that night, past silent, watchful walls and away from the village to the donkey left tethered at the river's edge. Papa mounted and reached down for me held high in Mama's arms. And we left her standing alone on an infinite plain under a knife-edged crescent moon.

We crossed the plain, wound up and over the pass, descended the mountains along oleander ravines vivid pink with promise, through pine forests heavy scented under a hot blue sky. We came, finally, to the end of land, to liquid blue which spoke, and soothed, and cooled. It was a cruel joke, this water, for while the smallest mountain stream tumbling from heaven could slake the thirst of multitudes, this water which stretched out before us could not serve so much as a simple drink.

We followed this false water and reached a city that gleamed beside the shore, threading our way through a clamour of donkeys, carts, and camels, coming at last upon a shop gleaming with silken colour. A man with greying hair and a red beard emerged from the shadows. He examined us with wonder. Did history repeat itself? Could this be? A lifetime ago — perhaps thirty years — he had sheltered a man who could have been my father, accompanied by a child who could have been me.

They spoke that night, low voices mingling with the rustle of leaves and the glimmer of stars, of that man, my grandfather, and the child, my mother, and of the world once again running red with the madness of war.

The next morning, as sea and sky were one in shimmering silver light, Papa left me. We watched, the red-haired man and I, as he followed the shore, playing in and out of the light. At the last bend, he turned and looked back, helpless against the light. I screamed, and ran after him. I fell. When I looked up, he was gone.

# I

## CITY OF A__

# CHAPTER 1

The air lay heavy on the city, a sticky coating on the world. That night, I woke up and looked out at the sky. The stars were far away, too far away to reach out to put one in your hair or hang on a string around your neck beside the cat's-eye and the cross. There was no moon.

I sat up on the bed. In my village, we had no beds, only felt carpets that hugged the earth. I got off and lay on my carpet. Mama had woven it, shapes and colours pouring from her fingers like a song. It was all she had, she said, all she could give. God knew, she said, she had always wished she had had something — anything, even a fork or a spoon — just to let her know that the first five years of her life were more than simply a story she told herself.

I fell asleep. I awoke to a hot and heavy sun. It wasn't a mountain morning.

The door opened.

It was my new "aunt." She didn't look like an aunt. My aunts wore sharwals, full flowing trousers gathered tight around the ankles, and full bright blouses. They were red-cheeked and strong. This aunt was short and round, like a small cooking pot, and old, like a grandmother, yet dressed as shameless women dressed, with hair uncovered, arms and legs bare. Nor was the man like one of my uncles, quick with laughter and quick with anger: he was old, fine, like a bent pencil, with patient grey eyes.

The man and the woman were talking to me. What was wrong? Why was I on the carpet? Why wasn't I in bed? I wanted to explain, I wanted to say that my carpet hugged the earth, that the earth was the floor, that lying beside me beyond the pine forests and blush-pink peaks were Mama and Papa. Instead, I listened as they told me in strangely accented Turkish that I would be as their own until Mama and Papa came for me — a few days, a few weeks — as long as it might take: I was theirs and no one could take me from them. I would be happy here. The country was preparing to enter the war, but that would not change life for children. I would go to school.

We didn't have "school" in my village, only lessons for the boys to read from the Koran and recite the prayers. But that was not "school": school was a place where children went so that they could take their place in the world, girls as well as boys, where they learned of numbers and words, of ancient times and faraway places.

I didn't want to go where there would be other children; other children were Turks, Muslim Turks, curs who threw rocks at infidels.

"There is no such thing as 'infidel' or 'cur,'" Aunt Gracia snapped. "There are only children, and some of them are Muslim, and some of them are Armenian. Or Jewish, or Greek, for that matter. What difference does it make?"

She was lying. I knew it. There were no other Armenian children. Mama had said there was only her and me left.

She held out navy slacks and a tunic and a white blouse and tried to make me take off the sharwals that Mama and I had made, carding and spinning the wool, weaving a soft white cloth, dying it yellow with onion skins — yellow like the sun, for I was my mother's sun. I curled up in a ball, and I wouldn't let her touch me. She left me in the room. I fell asleep.

But she came back, and now she had my new "cousin" with her dressed in the same tunic and white blouse. Mariam had large, soft, liquid black eyes, and smooth blue-black braids. I had hair that struggled out of braids and popped into curls. "You won't be able to learn if you don't go to school," Mariam said solemnly.

I didn't answer, and I didn't move.

They left.

Aisha Hanim, the helper, exactly like an aunt with hair modestly covered, bright sharwals, and rough strong hands, came in and led me out to the courtyard where Uncle Samuel sat with a dish of yoghurt and honey and a newspaper. He peered over his glasses. Today I would meet another Armenian.

"All the Armenians are dead," I said.

"Armenians are not so easy to get rid of," he said. "They've been in Anatolia for four thousand years, and they'll be here for another four thousand."

I followed Uncle Samuel down the dusty lane through the reflected light of whitewashed walls to the cobbled market square busy with camels and donkeys and sheep and goats, filled with bales of cotton and wool and mounds of beetroot and onion, baskets of fava beans, bundles of herbs. It was heaven's market place, the market place of Grandfather's stories, where a man sat from dawn to dusk with dishes of hazelnuts and raisins, with a *hubble bubble*, a water pipe, and tea (always hot and just sweet enough) and no matter how many sacks of barley or potatoes or beans were sold, still more remained.

He led me to the Armenian, a seller of carpets. He sat cross-legged on a pile of his carpets like a happy courtyard djinni, round and bald with heavy black eyebrows that danced as he spoke. He wore a heavy silver cross at his neck, not hidden, not one you could eat.

He had two names, "Zaven" and "Bedoukian." All Armenians, he said, had "ian," son of, at the end of their name, though not all had a name that belied their trade, for his name meant "the son of a potter." Yet here he was, a carpet seller. For me, though, he was only Ami, uncle. So many names at my age were not necessary. I was a lucky child — he had no uncles, Uncle Samuel had no uncles, and here I was, a little girl with not one but two. Who knew what other gifts life could bring?

No one in my village had a last name. I was just Zeyneb, daughter of Nazrat.

"You're an infidel," I said.

"First," he said, "there was Christ, and then there was Mohammed. I think the ones who came after should be the infidels, don't you?"

"All the Armenians are dead," I announced once more.

"Am I dead? Are you dead? Then we are two Armenians who are not dead. And your mother — that's three. And if there are three of us, who knows how many more there must be? In fact," he leaned in and whispered, "they say that in Jerusalem there are thousands of us, walking every day on the ground that Jesus walked."

I had never heard of "Jerusalem." Only Mecca.

He gave me his cross. That night, I took it out of my pocket and showed it to the moon.

The next day, Aunt Gracia tried to dress me again. I backed away from her, crouched in the corner of the room.

"All right," she said. "I give up. But you're going to school. Just don't come crying to me if the other children laugh at you."

She walked me up the hill to a long, low building with faded blue shutters, a lifeless blue that could protect no one. Everybody stared, all the girls in their navy pants and tunics and short-sleeved blouses, shameless, with bare arms, and all the boys, in neat navy pants and white shirts. I was led past all those staring eyes into a room filled with desks like a courtyard crowded with chickens so that you couldn't walk without being pecked. At the front, a long, thin, rumpled man was writing on the blackboard.

"She doesn't have a uniform," he said.

"You'll have to take her as she is," Aunt Gracia said.

The teacher shrugged. "There's no desk," he said. He turned back to the blackboard.

I had to sit with Mariam. I wanted to bite her.

School was awful. All the kids knew numbers and letters, but they weren't the long, lovely Armenian letters Mama had shown me, nor even the graceful Arabic letters of Papa's Koran. They were Turkish letters. Mariam knew everything, and I didn't know a thing. When the bell rang, and everyone went outside to skip or play five stones, I stood outside against the wall, and then I slipped away out of the gate and ran.

Uncle Samuel found me sitting on the shore. "What are you doing here?"

"Waiting for Papa," I said.

He took my hand.

"We'll wait at home."

The next morning, Aisha Hanim took me to school, grumbling up the hill about education being a waste of time, for boys as well as girls. It was the Koran that made an honest man, the Koran that was the bridge to heaven. She left me at the gate. I watched her disappear down the narrow lane, her long white head scarf a gleam of strength between shadowed walls. When Uncle Samuel found me at the river that evening, he didn't ask what I was waiting for.

This time, Aunt Gracia took me back to school herself.

"I send her to school to learn," she said to the teacher. "Not to sit."

The teacher waved his long thin arms at her, "What do you expect me to do? There is only one month of the school year left. Even Allah couldn't do what you ask."

"I'm not talking to Allah," she said. "I'm talking to you. I don't care what you teach her, but teach her something."

While the others were reading a story about a clever cat, he showed me how to draw letters, round a's, and o's and c's, and long l's and t's and j's. He helped me draw my name to take home to show Aunt Gracia and Uncle Samuel. But when he went away, I drew my secret name, the way Mama had drawn it on a glittering page of snow. That night, I held it up and showed it to the moon. I thought I saw the letters of my name hidden in the patterns on the moon. I thought I saw the cross.

One morning I didn't have to go to school: I wouldn't have to go back for three long months. I wouldn't have to feel eyes on my back, or sneak to the river. I would be free.

Aisha Hanim nabbed me on my way out the gate.

"Absolutely not," she said. "You're not leaving this courtyard."

"Why not?"

"Your aunt won't let you."

"Why not?"

"Ask her. She runs this ship."

I asked her.

"This isn't your mountain village," Aunt Gracia said. "Little girls don't wander the streets like any stray goat."

There were no stray goats. They all belonged to someone, and it was we children who had led them out to the slopes of the mountains in the morning and herded them back in the evening. I tried to tell her. She sent me to my room.

"Never argue with the captain," Aisha Hanim said.

The day was long. Long, lonely, and empty. Like the sky.

"How would you like to learn the silk trade?" Uncle Samuel asked one morning. "Money is like dirt on your hands that washes off with water. But a trade stays with you forever." He handed me a broom, one he had had made for me, my size and my beginning, he said, for with this broom, I would learn the secret of silk, how it brought life to a faded cheek or a line of pride to a young man's stance, how it complemented the dance in a young girl's eye.

"She's only seven years old," Aunt Gracia said. "What are you doing?"

"Teaching her poetry. To sell," he said, "one must reach the heart."

And so I had the freedom of the market square, and the poetry of the hawkers of sherbet and pistachios, of tomatoes and radios, filled the air. The buyers had their own lines of defence: "What? This heap of cobwebs which will come apart in my hand with the first wearing? May my children unto the seventh generation all be donkeys if I buy such a cloth." When the time came to cut, I handed Uncle Samuel the scissors.

As summer settled, the square emptied out after the early morning activity and doors were drawn shut against the midday heat. Even the scribe, who waited patiently under the large leaves of an almond tree beside his tray of pens and paper and ink, rolled out a carpet and fell asleep. One morning, instead of going with Uncle Samuel to learn the silk trade, Aunt Gracia handed me a shameless bathing suit. Aisha Hanim was aghast.

"At her age," Aunt Gracia said, "nothing is shameless. Put it on, Zeyneb. We're not in the middle ages."

Aisha Hanim pulled her scarf up over her hair and walked off in a huff.

Aunt Gracia was in a bad mood. Aunt Gracia was always in a bad mood whenever we had anything to do with Mariam's mother because Aimée was a daily and constant reminder of the mistake she had made when she sent her only son, a mere boy of nineteen, to France to visit Uncle Samuel's family. Who would have thought he'd come back with a wife? There were thousands of nice Jewish girls in Turkey, and he had to marry one who was *une française* who dressed like a whore. Everyone knew you could wear what you liked in the privacy of your courtyard, but that French woman cared nothing for whom she shamed.

In the privacy of her courtyard, Mariam's mother wore long flowing robes or sharwals of red or violet or emerald silk, but when she went to the beach she wore beach clothes and didn't see why children shouldn't as well. She and Mariam matched — short shorts and blouse — white with red polka dots. She'd made a set for me, too, so we all matched. I wanted to match.

"Over my dead body," Aunt Gracia said, climbing into the back seat of the car and plunking me on her lap. She said it in Turkish. Aunt Gracia spoke French well, but never to Mariam's mother, who still spoke terrible Turkish even after being in Turkey for almost ten years. Mariam's father Maurice poked his head in the back to kiss Aunt Gracia on the cheek. "Hello, you old goat," he said. He had Uncle Samuel's red hair and tease with Aunt Gracia's snapping black eyes. "Who shall we eat today?"

"You, if you're not careful," she said. "We never see you. How can you treat your mother that way?"

"I'm too busy saving rivers," he said. "That's why Aimée and I had Mariam. So you'd have a job."

"I don't need a job. Bringing you up was enough."

"Explain to me again, Ma, why Zeyneb can wear a bathing suit but not shorts?"

"Mind your own business," she said.

"Because it was my idea," Aimée said in French. "Why else?"

If Maurice hadn't been there, Aunt Gracia would have erupted. But she behaved better when he was there; he tamed her by removing Mariam privileges.

The next time we went to the sea, it was only Aunt Gracia and Uncle Samuel and Mariam and I. Maurice had gone to Ankara because the engineering department was worrying about the river silting up. Mariam's mother dropped us off and left us: she suddenly had to have her hair done. "How come Mariam has to come?" I said. We were sitting on the pebble beach. Silver-foam waves splashed up at us. "She has her own mother and father. Why does she have to come?"

"Zeyneb hates me," Mariam said, "and all anyone ever says is 'Poor Zeyneb this,' and 'Poor Zeyneb that,' and 'What lovely curls,' and 'What exquisite eyes.' No one ever calls me exquisite or feels sorry for me."

"She doesn't hate you," Uncle Samuel said.

"Yes, I do," I said.

"Gracia," Uncle Samuel called in desperation, "do something with these two. You know I can never do anything when our kids cry."

"What's going on?" Aunt Gracia demanded. She had been sleeping under her hat.

We told her.

"Stop it. You're both exquisite," she said. "I don't feel sorry for either one of you. You both have people who lose sleep over you. It would be like feeling sorry for — for pomegranates."

She sent us off over the pebble beach to look for sand to build palaces and tunnels. The sea sneaked in, silver blue over white sand, and ate them up. Uncle Samuel taught us to swim, floating on his back with each of us hanging on to a hand.

And then baskets of tomatoes and peaches had been canned, and the cobbled market square spilled over with mounds of grapes and olives and apricots and onions, and the noonday sun was a gentle, filtered light. School was starting.

We had a different teacher, Mr. Monzour, with short, stubby hands and a thick moustache like Papa's, and thoughtful eyes. This year, he said, I would learn to read. The world was full of books, and every book had something to tell us: books were djinn, waiting patiently for the day when they would be set free to wander in our imaginations.

He read to us from the book his father had read to him at our age, the one that had made him proud of being a Turk, proud of the mighty and benevolent Ottoman empire which for five hundred years had spread a mantle of peace over many and diverse peoples.

"I don't want to be a proud Turk," I said.

He sent a note home for Uncle Samuel.

"What do you want to be?" Uncle Samuel said.

"Nazrat's daughter."

"You can be many things and still be Nazrat's daughter."

Papa never read, though. Sometimes someone would bring a newspaper to the village and read it aloud, but he never read himself, not even the Koran, because Grandpa wouldn't allow one inside the courtyard walls: religion made people bloodthirsty.

"You don't have to read books that make you bloodthirsty," Uncle Samuel said. "Mr. Monzour is right. You never know when you open a book what kind of djinni will be inside. It might be a story about lazy Abdul or how silk came from China to Asia Minor. But once you open it and read it, it belongs to you. No one can take it away."

After that, I went to Mariam's as often as I could (even though Aunt Gracia said she'd live to regret the day she let me spend so much time there) because Mariam's mother had filled the entire house with books and magazines in French, Turkish, and English, and read to us about places where mountains were so high you could die, about fish the size of camels and women who shot lions. Mariam's mother didn't believe women had to be subservient wives. Even in France, a country one would expect to know better, women were abject, subservient wives. You had to admit that about Turkey at least, she said: here, in one of the most backward countries in the world, women sat as judges.

"Ha!" Aunt Gracia snorted. "Backward! The French live like pigs — bathe once a month if they have to — and she calls us backward. And who is she calling subservient? Me? Maurice treats her like a queen. Even Aisha Hanim isn't subservient, and she gets paid to be."

There were never any books or magazines about my village, though, never about a rushing spring river or angora goats in the sun.

I read at school, but I wouldn't do arithmetic. During arithmetic, I drew birds. This time, when Mr. Monzour sent the note home with me, I hid it. Aunt Gracia found it under Mama's carpet.

She looked puzzled.

"Why won't you do arithmetic?"

"It's not about anything," I said.

"It's not about anything? Sixty times a day, I hear, 'When will Papa come back?' 'How many more days of school?' and you're telling me arithmetic isn't about anything?" Weighing rice was arithmetic. Paying for rice was arithmetic. Measuring a carpet was arithmetic. The number of blossoms on a rosebush, the days we'd travelled from the mountains, the fishes in the sea, the stars in the sky...everywhere I looked, everything I saw, was arithmetic. Everyone every day of their lives did arithmetic. Papa did arithmetic. Mama did arithmetic. What made me think I was too good to do arithmetic?

Aisha Hanim had given me an onion and some feathers to count the moons, the number of times it came and went since Mama had taken my face in her hands, holding my face in her hands like a moon: "Remember," she said. "We live in a room lit by the moon. We're all together under the moon."

Every new moon, I stuck another feather into the onion. If I learned arithmetic, I wouldn't need an onion and feathers.

I preferred an onion and feathers. I liked to see what I was thinking.

Then Mr. Monzour taught us to play soccer, all of us, the boys and girls together. The boys didn't want to play with us: girls didn't do that. It was written in the Koran. "Don't be silly," Mr. Monzour said. "The Koran says girls and boys are to be treated equally. You're out of date."

"Not her, though," one of the boys said. It was Emek, the boy with green eyes. "I won't play with the goat girl."

He said it over and over, in the class when Mr. Monzour was writing on the board, in the yard when I was playing five stones or skipping: "Goat girl, goat girl, goat girl." One day, I got up out of my seat and kicked him. After school, I had to stay in to write lines: I will not kick Emek, I will not kick Emek, I will not... I drew pictures of birds instead, multicoloured bee-eaters and iridescent sunbirds not afraid to dip and flash in the sun. "Nice birds," Mr. Monzour said.

When he let me go, the others were waiting. Mariam was there, too. "Goat girl! Goat girl!" I ran. They followed me, calling after me. I fell. I hurt my hand on the sand and stone earth. I stood up and turned around, and I had a rock in my hand. "Goat girl!" I threw the rock. Blood flowed down Emek's forehead, trailed down his cheek, dripped onto his white shirt, bright red against pale skin, against a starched white shirt. His eyes were as green as a cat's. I picked up my pictures. They were crumpled. The sunbird was torn. When I turned to go home, no one followed. I walked down the dusty street to the river, past the creaking water wheel joyously spilling water back down to the earth. Beneath the surface of the river, the waterweeds waved, dark and green. I left my birds, torn and crippled, for the river.

Aunt Gracia was sitting under the grape arbour in the courtyard. She had a wooden spoon in her hand. "Where have you been?" she said. "What do you think you're doing, running around like any stray cat? You act like you're big enough to take care of yourself."

I ran up the outdoor stairs to the roof. She stood at the bottom of the steps, hands on her hips, waiting.

"If I have to come and get you, it's going to be twice as bad."

I didn't move.

"Aisha, go get her."

Aisha Hanim went to fold laundry.

When Uncle Samuel came home, the sun was setting over the white rooftops. He looked at me perched on the edge of the roof, and Aunt Gracia sitting on the bottom of the steps.

She burst into tears. "Why does she do this to me? I love her like my own. More than my own. Like the last rosebud, like a precious jewel..."

Uncle Samuel glared up at me. "You've been feeling sorry for yourself long enough! Come down right now, and kiss your aunt and tell her you're sorry — and you had better mean it!"

I came down and kissed her and said I was sorry. But I wasn't sure I meant it.

The next morning, I hid on the roof so I wouldn't have to go to school. Aisha Hanim found me. I said I was sick. She said she might believe me, but the captain wouldn't. The captain didn't: "No one is going to bother you at school," she said, "not after what you did. And not after I get through with them, believe me."

She took my hand and marched me up the hill. I had stones in my pocket, comfortable round ones I'd saved from the beach. I picked another one up on the way, a jagged one with the rose pink light of mountain peaks. The school was quiet. We were late. I could see the kids through the window, staring as we walked through the gate and across the sand and pebble yard.

The principal was standing in the hall. Aunt Gracia walked right by him. Mr. Monzour was in the middle of leading the allegiance to Turkey. "Where is that little murderer?" Aunt Gracia said.

He wasn't hard to find. He was the one with stitches on his forehead.

"Come up here, you," she said. He watched her. Unblinking. Terrified. He didn't move. She walked down the aisle and glowered down at him.

"Listen, you," Aunt Gracia said. "If you so much as even talk to my niece, you'll answer to me. You and your mother. Do you understand?"

I went to the seat I shared with Mariam. I didn't talk to her after that. I was never going to talk to her again. Emek and I were put on the same soccer team so that we would learn to cooperate. We didn't. I tripped him whenever I could, but no one could ever catch up to me because I'd think of Mama and Papa in the mountains, and I would run, back along the sea, up past the oleander ravines, through the pass, and down to our village. Then I would have to stay in and write lines: "A Turkish citizen does not hurt a player on his own team, A Turkish citizen does not hurt a player on his own team, A Turkish citizen does not..." I told Aunt Gracia I was staying in to do arithmetic. "Good," she said. "At last you're learning something."

In the afternoons, when Aisha Hanim thought I had been in school learning arithmetic long enough, she would come for me: I would look up from my notebook, and she would be standing at the gate, afraid to cross the courtyard, waiting until Mr. Monzour saw her and let me go. Finally, though, she strode across the yard, and lectured me through the window: What was this great mystery arithmetic? What good was school if it did nothing but make simple things difficult? Any farmer, any fisherman, any village simpleton, could explain it in less time than it took to peel an onion, and without this nonsense of pencil and paper. Arithmetic was nothing but ten, and if not ten, then it was half of ten, or half of half of ten. Everything began and ended with ten. Why did I think Allah had given me ten fingers and ten toes if not to understand that everything began and ended with ten?

She took a number larger than all of the seeds in a pomegranate and all of the lentils in a sack. She broke it down into tens, and halves of tens and halves of halves of tens, and multiplied it with another number she had broken down into tens and halves of tens and halves of halves, and added up the parts, and put back the zero at the ends. Zeros were nothing, she said, to be put in storage jars and taken back out when they were needed.

Mr. Monzour said if she did arithmetic that way, she was a genius and that while it was true that I needed to learn arithmetic, I had actually been staying in to learn something far more important in life: how to be a team player.

I learned to embroider that summer, egrets and herons, storks and cranes, the elegant birds that transformed into the flowing Armenian script. I sneaked tawny warblers into the corners, shy birds that sang without being seen.

With the blustery rains of the coming winter, Aunt Gracia was often in bed with her migraine headaches. On those days, when the whole world, river and sky, was like being inside a grey bottle, Aisha Hanim met me at the gate after school with a warm *borek*, and I would know that I was free. I would wander the cobbled streets and muddy lanes watching coppersmiths beating metal into shining shapes, leatherworkers cutting harnesses and blinders for donkeys and camels, weavers working colours and texture back into worn carpets. I would sit with the spice vendors surrounded by sacks of cinnamon, turmeric, cumin and mint, watching the grey rain fall. I made money. I waited at the coffee shop, my eyes fixed on the tangle of pewter and brass and clay bells, each one attached to a rope strung to a shop on the square.

The one who identified the bell won the right to deliver the coffee and the coin the shopkeeper gave in reward.

Uncle Samuel's bell had a high brass tinkle; the goldsmith's a laugh of gold. But the coins all jingled the same. Uncle Samuel sewed me a red silk pouch to receive my coins: "A full pouch never jingles," he said. "It is the man who has nothing who advertises his few poor coins."

I waited for there to be enough coins so that I could walk silently, important in my wealth.

Finally, the pouch was full. I walked across the market square to the barber. I climbed up onto the chair.

"I want to be a boy," I said.

"A barber cannot make you a boy. A barber can only make you a girl with short hair, and even this I cannot do. It is against the will of Allah."

"Allah doesn't care if I have short hair," I said. "I'm an infidel."

"Your uncle cares," he said.

"He wants me to be a boy," I said. "See?" I showed him my money. He cut my curls. I ran to show Uncle Samuel. "Look," I said. "I'm a boy."

"So?" he said.

"So now Aunt Gracia will let me run free like any stray goat."

"Is that so?" he said.

I ran home to show Aunt Gracia my cap of curls. I woke her up. "I give up," she said. "Just don't talk to me about goats."

At recess one day Emek did it again: "If Hitler thinks he has trouble with the Jews, look at what we have. Armenians and Jews." The other kids laughed. I took one of my stones out of my pocket. I drew my arm back to throw. They ran.

Mariam didn't. I played with my rock.

"Well? Aren't you afraid?"

"No," she said. "I'm sorry."

I bit my lip. I didn't want her to be sorry. I handed her the pink stone and walked to the river. Gulls stood on the shore, their shoulders hunched against the drizzle. Uncle Samuel found me. He picked me up and carried me home. I didn't want to go. I wanted to wait. Maybe Papa hadn't come back for me because I hadn't waited long enough. If I didn't wait, I would never go back to my mountains. I would never sit weaving colours in the courtyard with Mama, never be warmed by the sun shining through the crystal cool. It was never like that here, never crystal cool. Even winter wasn't real here. Nothing happened. I waited and waited for something to happen, but nothing ever did. Not one snowflake, no brilliant glittering light — just rain and gloom.

God didn't live here.

Once after Uncle Samuel came back from the synagogue and I came back from mass with Ami, I had asked, Where did God live? In church? The mosque? The synagogue?

God didn't live anywhere, he said.

Even Allah? I asked. Even Jesus?

Allah and God were the same, he said, and as for Jesus, if there was no God, who was Jesus?

Aunt Gracia had been angry — life was hard enough without God — and he had turned on her: "Wait till the war is over. Wait till they stop rounding people up like cattle for the slaughter. Then we'll talk about God. I'll talk about all gods then, any god you want. I'll pray and give thanks to all of them."

And he cried, suddenly, with such sobs as I had never heard.

"Yet we go on living," he said, "as though this were a day like any other. How can we go on living?"

My mother never knew why she lived, either. "For you," she whispered to me once. "Perhaps I lived to give life to you." But she hadn't cried. She had never cried.

Now I was gone. If I was gone, was Mama dead? And was Papa also dead because Mama was dead? All because I was no longer with them?

I felt tears run down my cheeks, watched as they dropped one by one, disappeared into the tears from the sky. I wanted it to be night and clear, so I could see the moon and I would know that Mama and Papa were still there. Sometimes, when Aunt Gracia didn't know what to do with me, she put me in my room and locked the shutters so that I couldn't see out. It was the punishment more terrible than any, not to be able to see the rooftops, the white gulls wheeling against the blue — not to see the moon and the stars. If the moon couldn't see me, Mama couldn't see me; if I couldn't see the moon, Mama and Papa were gone.

I screamed. I hid my face against Uncle Samuel's chest. I wet his shirt with my tears. I wanted to go back to the mountains and be dead with Mama and Papa.

He turned my face to his. What was this? A little girl who wanted to die? Who ever heard of such a thing? Did a mother and father die because their daughter is safe? No. They lived so that they might see her again.

When I went back to school Mr. Monzour talked about us being children of many nations, of the world being made of many nations, and if we thirty-four children couldn't get along, how did we expect the world to get along with its millions? From now on, he would be with us at recess, and Emek and I would sit on opposite sides of the room: if we didn't like each other, perhaps, out of sight, we would forget about each other.

We didn't. I still had my rocks in my pocket, and Emek knew it.

Christmas came. I wore my silver cross on top of my blouse so that everyone could see it, but I held Ami's hand tightly as we walked through a silent city under stars made distant by the humid winter night, past Emek's house, past

Mariam's, into the church with the Armenian cross over the door, a strong square cross with crosslets at each end. There were other children from school there, children with Turkish names — children who had said nothing when Emek called me infidel. We stood, and listened to the mass, and turned to kiss each other and give each other the news: Jesus was born.

When we walked home, it was raining again. There would have been snow in the mountains, soft and silent under felt boots. There would be a silent immense sky over a silent immense land, a silence so large that the stories of God and Allah and Jesus seemed true.

And then there was Aunt Gracia and Uncle Samuel's holiday, a festival of lights, one more candle lit each day, until eight candles burned bright against a cold, wet night. Spring came. Finally, school closed for Ramadan, and the muezzin's voice rang out over the city and sang to the sky. In the day, Mama and Papa and the mountain plain were lost in the sunlight, but in the night, in dream, we laughed and spoke.

Then, one night, I saw Mama standing as we had left her, alone on an infinite plain under a knife-edged crescent moon.

The next night, the plain was empty, and the moon was large.

I woke and looked out. There was a full moon. I went to Aunt Gracia and Uncle Samuel's room. I slept on the floor beside their bed under the moonlight.

The third night, Papa was in my dream. He knelt, and looked into my eyes with all the tenderness of the spring sun: I felt the strength of his arms and his breath on my cheek. And then he was gone.

I woke up screaming. I woke up as Mama so often had. Mama and Papa were dead.

# CHAPTER 2

Aisha Hanim said it was a false sunrise. Aunt Gracia said she would take what she could get: I was good, docile as a kitten, gentle as a dove. After school, I played with Mariam, and we played what she wanted — princesses. Mariam was always the princess whose beauty drew humble servants and princes from far corners of the empire, from Samarkand to Salonika, to seek her hand in marriage. I was the suitor who won her by cutting off dragons' heads and descending deep, hot wells; I was clever Hodja who could trick anybody, even the sultan, into anything. I tricked him into letting her marry me. We lived happily ever after.

Then one day Father Havonissian, the Armenian priest, was hovering at the door of Uncle Samuel's shop. He said something to me in Armenian, and when I didn't understand, he turned on Uncle Samuel: "What did I tell you? She is nothing. Worse than nothing."

That night, I heard Uncle Samuel telling Aunt Gracia that I was worse than nothing.

"I hope you threw him out," Aunt Gracia said.

"He's an old man. How could I throw him out?" Uncle Samuel said. "He's worried about her, that's all."

"Ha!" Aunt Gracia said. "As if she doesn't know too much about being Armenian already. Does he think it's easy, that we do it for fun? Where does he get the right to tell us we have no business bringing her up? What makes him think he can do any better?"

I didn't want to play princesses after that. We played infidels and curs, and Mariam was always the infidel, and I killed her. She ran to Aunt Gracia: she wanted to kill me back. Aunt Gracia threw up her hands. "Is that what you want to be when you grow up? Murderers? What kind of children are we raising?"

"I don't like her games, anyway," Mariam said. "All her games are dead games." She went home. Aunt Gracia sent me to Uncle Samuel's shop. "Go learn to make money," she said. "At least that will be useful."

I asked Ami if I was worse than nothing. "Worse than nothing?" he said. His eyebrows danced in horror. "You are more than everything." He was lying. No one could be more than everything, more than the mountains and the moon, more than an orange-winged butterfly and a bright pink flower, more than the darkness and the light. That night, I dreamed, and it was me under the moon, alone on an empty plain. I sat under the moon, and I cried. Papa had begged Mama to come: the donkey could carry all three of us, he said; she was light as a feather, and I was less than nothing; he would walk... She had stood, silent, helpless.

"Why, Papa?" I said. "Why won't she come?"

"I don't know why," he said. He was angry.

"Isn't she afraid?" I said.

"We are all afraid," he said. "So what?"

In my dream, I walked toward her, but she shook her head, held up her hand to stop me. She backed away, terrified, trying not to show panic, trying not to frighten me. I turned and suddenly from behind me the children from the village appeared, rising out of the fields of rippling wheat. In a fury, they swarmed over her scattering blood and bone over the plain. Her eyes were blue flowers in the plain. Small hand scythes lay scattered like stars. I screamed and called for Papa. Something stirred at my feet. It was Papa, covered in blood with open, surprised eyes, brown eyes as deep as the earth.

I woke up terrified. I was afraid to go back to sleep. I didn't want to see Mama and Papa die. If only I could keep awake, they wouldn't die.

The next day, Mariam's mother brought me a box of paints. If you paint your dreams, she said, and sit with them in front of you, they aren't inside of you anymore. You can leave them behind on the table, throw them into the fire. But I was afraid that if I painted them, my dreams would be real, and if I forgot, I would forget Mama and Papa.

Mariam wouldn't paint either. She wanted to keep her dreams, all of them.

"I give up," Aunt Gracia said. "Go to the market. That's where you want to be, anyway."

The square was quiet. Everyone had congregated around Uncle Samuel's shop to listen to the news on the radio — Father Havonissian, Ami Zaven, the barber, the goldsmith, the tinsmith, the herb seller, the shoemaker, the scribe, the weaver, the coffee seller, the hawkers. Turkey was entering the modern era. We would have roads into the interior as far as the Russian border. We would have the vote. The day of starvation on the plateaus would be over; each man would have the power of a sultan.

Father Havonissian laughed. They treated us like children, expecting us to forget that roads brought soldiers as well as food, expecting us to forget that Hitler had been voted into power. What good had the vote done the millions who had died by his hand, or the millions who were dying to stop him? What good would that vote have done the one and a half million Turkish Armenians who had died in 1915? What good would the vote have done the thousands of Greeks who died in the expulsion from Turkey in 1923? And what would happen if those for whom we voted should not obey our wishes? How would we punish them? And would each of us simple men with the power of a sultan now have enough fuel for our stoves? Cloth for coats? Shoes for our children? Kerosene for our lamps? We were not so stupid, we simple men, that we did not understand that if the Americans did not want access to our Russian border, this gift of trucks and roads, this vote designed to prove we were like them, would disappear tomorrow. Yet America did not need to buy our hatred of Russia — Turkey had hated Russia at least since World War I for thieving our oil and our territory. Even Turkish Armenians, since the Armenian Republic had been subjugated by Russia, hated Russia.

Hooded crows, tan and black, pecked at blue flowers on the plains.

Now when Mariam and I played, we were tragic princesses. We dug into Aunt Gracia's trunk filled with veils and long gowns and sharwals, rejecting the lustrous silks worn within the courtyard for the heavy black cottons and wool yashmaks, the cloak-veils, for forays outside the harem. Pulling our yashmaks over our faces, we escaped the confines of the palace for the first time in our lives and rejoiced in alleys, lanes, shadows, dust, and dirt.

We saw men. They walked freely, unfettered, unashamed; their faces were lifted to the light. Except for our father the sultan, we had never seen a man; not even the eunuchs, who we knew guarded the women's palace, were allowed within our walls. One day one of these men, struck by the beauty of our eyes, would recognize our royal blood and fall at our feet, desperate to rescue us from our empty, lonely lives.

We took tea with trusted shopkeepers.

We were examining new carpets for the royal quarters when Father Havonissian appeared, black robes in a swirl.

Silence fell as he stood in the square, a still dark centre under a hot eastern sun, and spoke as though he were discussing the price of peaches. There were Commandments which we all shared, we peoples of the book, yet somehow we all behaved as though these Commandments were meant only for our families, our friends. While God, Allah, and Jesus had room for all who came, we had no room at all. Why else would a mother be murdered for no greater crime than memory? Why would her husband have been murdered for no greater crime than that he loved her? Were our memories and our love so dangerous?

He waited for an answer.

"Oh," Mariam said airily, too busy being a princess to hear. She pulled her yashmak up over her face, "that foolish Armenian priest again. We'll have to tell the Sultan that infidels roam the marketplace."

I shook off my veil and slipped out. The sun was shining. The sea wind was fresh. The salt air was sharp and alive. I was alive.

It was odd to be alive when other people were dead.

In my room, I locked the shutters, blocking out the emptiness of the sky. Aunt Gracia came to see what was wrong.

"I'm alive," I said.

"Thank goodness for that," she said. "There's been too much death in the last thirty years already."

Uncle Samuel came home. He was sorry, he said, sorry for life, sorry for death, sorry for my dreams, sorry for the world. But now I would no longer wait, and perhaps I would no longer dream.

I lay awake the whole night and the next day afraid to sleep. I didn't want to get up, and I didn't want to eat. Aunt Gracia said I was going to be the death of her. Aisha Hanim gave me another cat's eye. Mariam cried. When Uncle Samuel came back from the shop that evening, I was still on the floor.

"Get up," he said.

I lay there.

"Let me tell you something," he said. "You think you will lie there and die quietly, but it isn't so easy to die. And even if it was, your mother and father sent you to us to live."

"I don't want to," I said.

"Who are you to deny them their gift? Life isn't so bad. Now get up."

I got up. Aunt Gracia sat me at the table and slammed a dish of yoghurt down in front of me.

"Eat," she said. "There's no point in being tragic now. You knew they were dead."

"But I'm an orphan," I said.

I had read plenty of stories about orphans, spending their lives carrying water and spinning and sweeping until they died.

"Don't you dare compare yourself to those orphans," she said. She cuffed me on the side of the head. "When your uncle and I lose sleep over you at our age. Do I deserve this?"

At school, I was no longer good. The teacher put me in the corner, he made me write lines, he kept me in, and, finally, when he caught me drawing mean pictures of everyone, he slapped my hands with a ruler in front of the whole class. Mariam watched and cried. Aunt Gracia had hysterics. Father Havonissian prayed.

Mama had talked to Jesus. He hadn't helped her.

"This is what comes," Father Havonissian said, "of living with the *odar*, with strangers."

"*Odar*? Stranger?" Uncle Samuel said. "How can you say that to me? When I have cried for your people and you for mine? You're fooling yourself if you think you're fighting for her soul. Zeyneb is not your answer to genocide and to war. You're fighting for one and a half million Armenians who are never coming back. Your people. Mine. They're never coming back. Whether one little girl speaks Armenian or not isn't going to bring them back."

Suddenly, Father Havonisian looked older than the earth.

"We're dying," he said. "As surely as though we were still being slaughtered in the streets. My congregation steals into the church like thieves, they're afraid to speak to me in the streets, they hide behind Turkish names. Even this —" he looked at his robe, patched and mended, threadbare and worn. "When I wear this I break the law."

I didn't go to mass with Ami that Christmas. I sat on Mama's carpet and wound blood-red threads around my wrists. But I didn't say any prayers.

We had a new teacher after the February break, Miss Sehoglu, with eyes like the evening sky and long dark hair piled up on her head. She was quick and small and she wore flower colours, buttercup yellow and forget-me-not blue. Miss Sehoglu was excited by everything. Science was life, she said. Mathematics was an explanation of mystery. Words were everything we could know or imagine. Music was the voice of the universe. Drawing, no matter what old teachings said, did not capture the soul, but revealed it. I drew waterwheels splashing in the sun, chameleons hiding in bougainvillea vines. I drew a courtyard, and a rushing spring river. Somewhere, in the Anatolian plateau was a village near a rushing spring river — somewhere, lost in my memory.

We learned about the story of life, of beetles and rats, and flowers and man. Evolution. The survival of the fittest.

Survival of the fittest was why all the Armenians were dead. Mama had been right when she had said, "I wasn't meant to live."

"Come on," I said to Mariam. "Before it's too late." I pulled her after me, running all the way home to tell Aunt Gracia that Miss Sehoglu was going to kill all of us, Armenians and Jews alike. Anybody who could be killed was supposed to be because they could be. It was the rule.

"Mariam," Aunt Gracia said. "You're sensible. What's she talking about?" Mariam didn't know. Uncle Samuel took us back to the school. I saw Miss Sehoglu through the window, waiting. "She wants to kill us," I said. "See? She's waiting."

"Don't be silly," Uncle Samuel said. "Look at her. She looks like she's going to cry."

It was true. She did.

"Maybe you didn't understand what she said."

But I had. I knew I had. I made her tell him what she had said. Survival of the fittest had changed the idea of creation. It was the opening up of science, of understanding life on earth. Survival was the law of nature. The strong survive. Nature did not like weaklings.

"See?" I said.

"Her mother was Armenian," Uncle Samuel explained. "She thinks you're saying that nature meant the Armenians to die because they are the weak."

"That's ridiculous. Armenians aren't weak! They started a civil war."

"Are you talking about the massacres?" Uncle Samuel said.

"There were no massacres," Miss Sehoglu said.

"You are young," he said. "It was before your time."

"Yes, it was. But I know. There were no massacres. The Armenians rebelled. They wanted to break away and form their own country, and they did it during World War I when we had other things to worry about. The Armenians got what they deserved, believe me."

Uncle Samuel listened as she told him how the civil war had started, how we had attacked one of our own villages and blamed it on the Turks.

"Why would they have done that?" Uncle Samuel said.

"To get world sympathy. They were hoping that the allies would force us to allow them to secede. They started a civil war that they couldn't win. And they haven't given up with their lies. They are very precise, the Armenians. They have a date, April 24, 1915, and a telegram: 'all Armenians, the old, the sick, to be killed without mercy.' But there was no such telegram. It's a forgery — Armenian propaganda to turn the world against us."

She had the books. Not just Turkish books, German as well. German scholars wrote of this. Right from the beginning, the Armenians had run for help to the German military advisors stationed in Turkey. And right from the beginning, the Germans had seen through the Armenian lies.

"The new Turkish curriculum also teaches that all languages descend from Turkish," Uncle Samuel said. "But if the most civilized nation in the world supports you, what can I say?"

We left. It was a sparkling day, both warm and cool, sun and blue. In the distance, the river glittered the blue of Mama's eyes.

"Is she right?" I said. "Didn't the Turks want us dead?"

"She's half right. Not all Turks wanted you dead. Your mother wasn't the only child taken in by the Turks. Armenian families were hidden by them. But the Turkish government of the time did."

"Mama said God wanted us dead."

"You can't confuse what people want with what God wants."

Survival of the fittest, he said, was about the evolution of animals before reason, dinosaurs, and flying lizards, and whales. Man was no longer an animal that thought only about getting enough to eat and lying in the sun. Man had reason, and man had learned that everyone had the right to life — to eat, to sleep, to raise their children, and to die in peace. We had choices. While animals could do only what they were born to do, man could learn new ways.

Aunt Gracia wasn't impressed by survival of the fittest. "That's new?" she said. "The strong have been killing the weak throughout the ages. We need a rule to tell us this?"

"Uncle Samuel says man is an animal of reason," I said.

"Your uncle is a dreamer," she said.

"The world was built on dreams," Uncle Samuel said. "By dreamers."

"Ha!" she said.

Neither Mariam nor I went back to school. We weren't going back until the following year when we wouldn't have Miss Sehoglu. Mariam's mother taught us.

The next time we dressed in Aunt Gracia's veils, we were wives of the sultan trying to escape the harem because the sultan's mother was plotting the murder of our babies. If she succeeded, Mariam would drown herself in the bathing pool in the women's garden, and the next time the sultan called me to his bed I would strike him in the heart with his own golden dagger. I would have to stab myself to death afterwards, of course; otherwise, I would be stoned, and that would be worse. But it didn't matter because I deserved to be dead. Mama and Papa were dead. They were dead because of me and the sign of the cross.

"Don't flatter yourself, Zeyneb," Aunt Gracia said, "that you are responsible for the evil of the actions of others."

Uncle Samuel blew up.

"There şhe goes wishing herself dead! She's as thin as a broom. What's the difference between her and the people coming out of the concentration camps? Do you know what your mother looked like by the time your grandfather brought her to me? Nothing but eyes. A bundle I could hold in my hand. If you're not careful, you're going to give them exactly what they want, and that's another dead Armenian. Thousands of Armenians died fighting back. What right do you have to lie down and die without a fight?"

He came after me. I ran out to the courtyard and up the steps to the roof. Uncle Samuel looked up at me on the roof, and then he slumped onto the step. Aunt Gracia glared up me. "Look what you're doing to your uncle!"

"I don't care," I said. "You're going to give me away, anyway."

"I'd love to give you away," she said. "No one would have you."

"Because I'm Armenian?"

"Because you never give me a moment's peace. What makes you think you're any different just because you're Armenian?"

"Mama and Papa gave me away."

"They didn't give you away. They saved your life. What do you think we're trying to do? If you don't stop with your killing and dying, I'll kill you myself. I promise you."

I promised to stop with my killing and dying.

Father Havonissian brought sugared almonds for my birthday. It was spring. The storks were back. There were new leaves on the grape vines, and the pots of roses showed buds. Father Havonissian said he hoped I knew that Mama and Papa were happy — free of their suffering — together in heaven with God.

I knew that wasn't true. Heaven was only a dream to keep you warm when you were caught in the mountain passes, a dream where camels were good-natured, standing up when you wished, kneeling down when you wished, always agreeable when fed only a dry bush once a year. My grandfather had given his respect to the sun: "I don't ask more than the sun can give, but I give my thanks all the same, without expecting more because of my thanks. I thank the sun because it is good to know what is good."

"She's a heathen," Father Havonissian said. He sighed and reached for an almond. "Well, I suppose it could be worse."

Uncle Samuel brought out tea, stirred sugar into crystal cups. "We are two old men," he said, "who both know that we spoke to our God in any and every way we knew how — and it did no good."

After dinner, we sat on the roof. In the distance, the water wheel creaked.

# Chapter 3

I started to menstruate. I ran to tell Aunt Gracia. She was sitting on the roof in the centre of a carpet of apricots that had been pitted and laid out to dry. The river rippled and glittered in the distance.

"No. Can't be. You're too young. I haven't told you anything yet."

"I already know," I said. "Mariam's mother told us."

"Oh," she said. She looked relieved. "Well, you had to grow up sometime. We'll have to go to the baths this week. It's time to start finding you a husband."

Every mother at the baths kept an eye out for prospective daughters-in-law. As we were steamed, massaged and rinsed, in between chatter and towels, we were pronounced to have the smooth roundness of white doves, the sweetness of sugar, the quickness of swallows. We were the sweetest of angels, obedient, a blessing to any mother-in-law in her old age.

I didn't want a mother-in-law. I didn't want to menstruate. I didn't want to be able to have babies. When Mariam and I talked about it, it was always her getting married, having babies, and me being godmother. Mariam's babies lived and grew up.

"Nobody lets their parents find them husbands anymore," I said.

"If a sheep jumped off a cliff, would you jump, too? For thousands of years we have been finding our daughters husbands, and suddenly 'nobody does it anymore.' I never should have let you spend so much time with Mariam's mother. You used to be so sweet. Now look at you."

She was referring to the pedal pushers I was wearing which showed "everything I had": I had no respect for myself and I dressed like any common hussy. People would think I didn't have a family who cared enough about me to arrange a respectable marriage.

Yet at least once a week, Uncle Samuel teased Aunt Gracia about being a poor wandering traveller on his way to reclaim deserts for a dream of a New Jerusalem, brought home for dinner by her father only to be corrupted by her wanton eyes. She had seduced him over the soup with her eyes. Then she had sneaked out of the house wearing the helper's yashmak to meet him. What could her father do after such shameful behaviour? After this, who else would marry her? Aunt Gracia would erupt with a lecture on the ignorance of Europeans who thought that Middle-Eastern women were traded off like sheep. Had it never occurred to him that families visited and that children played together? Did he think that the girls were so bloodless that they wouldn't find a chance to drop their veils and flirt? Or that mothers wouldn't advance a son's cause by sending him to borrow a tablecloth or return a candle? When everyone shared the same streets, went to the same mosques, churches, and synagogues, how many strangers did he think there were?

"You weren't matched," I said. "Why do I have to be?"

"You've been listening to Sammy," she said. "He doesn't know what he's talking about."

I asked Mariam's mother to adopt me.

"Pumpkin," she said, "there's nothing I can do. Try somebody who didn't take her son away from her. In fact, try her son."

"Ma," Maurice said. "What's happened to you? You're turning back the clock. No one has been married off at fourteen in Turkey since before the days of Ataturk."

She told him to mind his own business. She wasn't making the mistake with me that she had made with him.

"The Behar boy," Aunt Gracia announced a week later. She had just come home from the baths. "He's in business with his father. You'll have a good life." The Behars were in silk, too, only in a bigger way than Uncle Samuel. The Behars had land with mulberry trees. They raised and harvested their own silkworms, from culling leaves to feeding the worms, to removing the silk from the cocoon, to spinning, weaving, and dyeing. They experimented with weaves and finishes to increase weight, drape, and sheen. They exported. I worked for them sometimes, cutting up the mulberry leaves and feeding the worms, thousands of munching worms growing before my eyes. They sounded like rain.

"He's a good boy," Aunt Gracia said.

The Behar boy was twelve years older than me. I didn't think the Behar boy had any idea who I was — just another wispy girl among bunches of women feeding worms.

"Why me?" I asked.

"Because his mother and I promised each other when we were girls. If anything ever happened to either of us, we would take each other's children."

I had a dream that night. It was me in my pedal pushers. I was lying on the open plain. A bundle wrapped in Mama's headscarf lay beside me. It was a baby. My baby. A dead baby. My baby was dead. In the distance, a man sat under the shadows of Aunt Gracia and Uncle Samuel's grape arbour. I couldn't see his face. I didn't know who he was. I got up and walked past him toward the mountains. I walked, and I walked — and then I ran.

I told Mariam my dream. She gasped. "You left your husband and your baby?"

"I'm not supposed to have babies."

"But Zeyneb," she said. "It's normal."

"Not for Armenians," I said.

Aunt Gracia was inviting the Behars over. I had always thought that Mrs. Behar was just another of Aunt Gracia's bath friends, a voice in the steam. "You can't," I said. "I have volleyball practice. We have a tournament coming up. We might even win this year."

"Good. I'll invite them to the game."

"That's not fair. How do you expect me to play well with people imagining me married?"

She did bring them to the game, Mr. and Mrs. Behar and Nissim, three matching mushrooms plumped on a bench watching me. We lost. Afterwards, I had to go over and be polite. I raised Aunt Gracia's and Uncle Samuel's and Mrs. Behar's hands to my forehead and didn't look at Nissim. When they came home for coffee with us, he walked up the hill exactly as a round brown mushroom would. Puffing.

"Go and change," Aunt Gracia whispered. She was showing off my embroidered birds framed on the wall. "Put on that pretty yellow batwing blouse and your full skirt."

I knew why she wanted me to change: it showed off my small waist and made me look like I had breasts and hips, and it got me out of the way so she could lie behind my back: I made the flakiest, most delicate pastry in all of the Near and Middle East, the most fragrant fillings with just the merest hint of rosewater. My preference, she said, was pistachio. I could hear Mrs. Behar across the courtyard gushing about how well I had turned out. So polite. So well trained. Such a hard worker. Young women today were not at all interested in anything but showing off. Why even Ataturk's daughter — she was adopted, too, you know — flew an airplane.

"Zeyneb can never sit still," Aunt Gracia agreed graciously. "She's always up to something."

I went down to the river. It was getting dark. The water wheel creaked. The date palms stood black against the sky. I wished that I could pray. I wished God and Jesus and Allah weren't men.

Uncle Samuel found me. "Aren't there any women I can pray to?" I said.

"Mary," he said.

"Mary won't understand," I said. "She had a baby."

He sent me to Mariam's mother.

"Pumpkin," she said. "You are a goddess. You don't need to go further than yourself."

She handed me a book. At one time, everybody in the civilized world, Greater Armenia, the Greek and Romans, worshipped gods and goddesses. The world had been a matriarchy, and the most powerful of all was Artemis.

Artemis. That was me. Artemis. Arta. Artemis hunted, she was chaste, and she controlled the moon.

I, Zeyneb, had avoided the moon. When the moon was full, Zeyneb closed the shutters. If she had to go out, she didn't look up. If she had a dream with the moon in it, she woke up. But Arta wasn't afraid of the moon. Arta remembered Mama saying we were all together under the light of the moon. Arta could fall asleep in the light of Mama and Papa in the patterns in the moon.

The next day, I went to volleyball practice and felt safe. Arta was chaste. Arta was powerful. No one would marry me, ever.

It was at volleyball practice that I found out that I was getting married.

"Why is she marrying you to the Behar boy?" Ami said. "She should be marrying you to an Armenian. We can't afford to have our blood thinned."

I gave Aunt Gracia the message.

"Just where does he expect me to find you an Armenian husband?" she stormed. "Every Armenian family that could, fled during the massacres, and the ones left behind are afraid to even admit they're Armenian. And no wonder."

"Let Mariam marry him," I said. "She wants to get married. That's all she ever talks about."

"If she were my daughter, believe me, I would, but she's not. She has that mother. Besides, the oldest always marries first. What are you trying to do to me? I have high blood pressure. All I'm trying to do is see you settled before I go. Is that a crime?"

Mariam would have made a perfect wife: she never gave a moment's trouble, she was pretty, and she had round, full womanly breasts. Mine were squingy skinny-girl breasts. The baby in my dream had probably starved to death. None of Mariam's babies would ever starve.

"It's not fair," I said.

"You're wasting your time if you expect life to be fair," Aunt Gracia sighed. "We each have to do the best with what we've got. And what you've had isn't so terrible. You're not stupid, you're attractive enough to make a good match, and even if you weren't, you have an old respected name."

When they adopted me, I became Zeyneb Gracia Mendes Reijskind. Aisha Hanim didn't speak to Aunt Gracia for a month because all these names were obliterating my Muslim roots, although exactly how this was doing it, even I couldn't see. I was still "Zeyneb," and I hadn't had a surname. My grandfather had refused to take a surname, no matter what edict Ataturk laid down: surnames simply allowed governments and armies to catalogue men for their own purposes.

Aunt Gracia had wanted Mariam to be named after her when she was born, but Mariam's mother hadn't allowed it. In France, Jews named their children for the dead. To have given Mariam her name would have been like wishing Aunt Gracia dead. Aunt Gracia hadn't forgiven Aimée: in Turkey, everyone, Armenian, Muslim, and Jew, named their children after the living, blessing them with life. If her mother-in-law's blessing wasn't good enough for her, she could always think of the name as that of Aunt Gracia's dead Spanish ancestor's name, Dona Gracia Mendes, a woman who had dedicated herself to Turkish Jewry and had a synagogue named for her in Istanbul. Dona Gracia Mendes had been delivered from the hands of the Spanish inquisition (she had been betrayed by her own daughter, but that was another story) by the intercession of Suleiman the Magnificent. Dona Gracia Mendes used her influence at court to intercede with the Sultan for Turkey's Jewry. How could it be bad luck to pass on the name of such a selfless woman?

"A bit of selflessness wouldn't hurt you, either," she said to me. "You could start worrying about someone else for a change. It's bad enough you're trying to drive my blood pressure up, but have you taken a good look at your uncle lately? He's not getting any younger. Neither of us is."

It was true. Aunt Gracia's skin had become fine parchment wrinkles and her hair was completely white. She was shorter than me now, too, and I was barely 152 centimetres tall.

I dragged Mariam with me to take a good look at Uncle Samuel. He was peering over his glasses, cutting a length of silk with stiff arthritic fingers. He had a bald spot, and there wasn't even a hint of red left in his beard.

"What's going on?" he said.

"Uncle Samuel," I said. "You're old."

"Is that so? Then I'm a lucky man. Where I come from, not so many have had the privilege. You should be happy for me. What else can you do? Get old for me? Die for me? Go find someone still young enough to help. Knit socks. Make soup for the hospital."

Mariam had an idea. It came to her while she was feeling sorry for me because I was an orphan. "Orphans," she said. "We can adopt orphans. After you get married, you can adopt some, and I'll help, and then when I get married, I'll adopt."

Ami Zaven had been a real orphan, one who when he was five years old had slept under stairways and in doorways. Unlike my mother, he had been rescued by no one, not until the genocide was well and truly over. Until then, the shopkeepers on the square fed him clandestinely, and when, miraculously, Father Havonissian re-emerged, he had lived with him. He hadn't expected to be adopted, though: God gave only one set of parents, and when they were gone, there weren't any more. His concern had been a bare bottom and cold feet. He retrieved a threadbare pair of trousers from a drawer in a small inlaid desk at the back of the shop and showed them to us. They had been chosen with thought for a young boy's future, with a belt that could be loosened and legs that could be turned down.

Ami dreamed still of the day he had received those trousers. In his dream, the shopkeeper also gave him two pairs of wool socks, one for him and one for his younger brother. He awoke, desperate to find his brother and give him the socks.

We didn't know any orphans to give clothes to. There were children who grew up with other families because their own parents couldn't afford to take care of them, but no real orphans. Emek's family was bringing up two other children. Aisha Hanim had been raised by another family. Aisha Hanim had promised herself when she married that she would have no more children than she could care for. With Allah's help, she had had only one child, a son.

Aunt Gracia said it had nothing to do with Allah. Aisha Hanim hadn't taken any chances. The only man she had agreed to marry was a sailor who put in to shore once a year, and when he did come home, she took herbs. Aisha Hanim might have been better off if she had had more children, because the one she had was a failure with a social conscience who believed that it was his duty to bring literacy to the mountains. He was in a village so poor that his classroom had neither windows nor fuel. He starved. He spent days in bed in the winter to keep warm and thought nothing of it because, after all, why should he, the teacher, live better than his pupils? Aisha Hanim could only wait for the day when he would come to his senses and realize that Allah meant him to take care of his mother rather than waste his time on strangers.

"Do they have to be orphans?" Aunt Gracia asked. "What about all the people coming out of Europe with nothing but the clothes on their backs?"

So Mariam and I started telling everyone about orphans coming out of Europe with nothing but the clothes on their backs who had to sleep under stairways half naked, and by the time the winter rains set in, we had a room full of clothes: men's, women's, and children's; cotton, linen, silk, and wool; pants, shirts, sweaters, and skirts. Mariam learned to knit. During volleyball games, Aunt Gracia and Mariam knitted socks.

At the baths, Aunt Gracia announced that Mariam and I were giving up all our spare time to work for others and that we had become so soft-hearted that we wouldn't let the maids lift a finger. Mrs. Behar looked at me with proprietary eyes, me and my perky little breasts. I stopped going. On the cold clammy days when Aunt Gracia and Mrs. Behar were enjoying steam, heat, conversation, and tea, I soaked in the tub at home. The dash across the courtyard to my room was invigorating.

The Behars came over again, three fat brown mushrooms. Nissim Behar raised Aunt Gracia and Uncle Samuel's hands to his forehead in the devout fashion that Aunt Gracia mourned had been lost in today's young people. This time she said I had cooked the entire meal. I didn't say a word the whole evening, not through the almonds and dates, or the lamb soup, or the pilaf, or the halvah, or the coffee. Neither did he. Mrs. Behar said she could see that I was settling down. Marriage always helped young people settle down.

"Well?" Aunt Gracia said after they left. "Isn't he a nice boy?"

"How would I know?" I said. "He never squeaked."

"He's respectful," she said. "Well brought up."

"He doesn't have any personality."

"He doesn't need any. You have enough for both of you. That's one of the things they like about you. He's shy. You'll help draw him out."

The next time Aunt Gracia came home from the baths, she reported that Mrs. Behar could talk about nothing but what wonderful girls Mariam and I were. Not only that, the rabbi's wife had asked the rabbi to commend us at a Friday night service.

In my dream that night, my baby was still dead, and I still couldn't see my husband's face, but when I got to the riverbank, I found a boat. I rowed through the reed-banked river down to the sea. I was free.

I awoke and went up onto the roof to watch the dawn. The light touched the smoky grey of the water with apricot and rose. Long-legged water birds poked at the edges. Gulls floated on a smooth expanse of light.

Uncle Samuel climbed up to join me. He stopped twice to catch his breath.

"Uncle Samuel, can't you make her stop?"

"Once Gracia gets an idea into her head," he said, "you just have to let it wear off. She'll get used to her high blood pressure, she'll see she's not going to die, and she'll forget about it."

"I don't know what's the matter with her. What's going to happen when Mrs. Behar finds out Aunt Gracia was lying about me? She'll probably come after her with an axe."

I met Father Havonissian on the street. He was stooped and shrunken now, too, almost Aunt Gracia's height, with a white beard and permanent worry wrinkles. He said he would talk to her for me. I didn't think it would do any good.

"Madame Reijskind," he said. "She is only a child."

"Ha!" she said. "Would she be only a child if she were marrying an Armenian?"

"She doesn't want to be married," he said. "Even to an Armenian."

"She doesn't know what she wants. She's only fourteen."

"Ah! You see? We are agreed that she is too young to know what she wants. Give her time. Maybe one day she will want to marry this boy."

"Don't play games with me," Aunt Gracia said. "You would never agree to her marrying a non-Armenian. Why are you torturing me?"

This time in my dream when I got to the open sea I jumped out of the boat and became a fish, free to swim in a silent blue world. The next time Aunt Gracia served fish, I wouldn't eat it. "Armenians don't eat fish," I said.

"They do if they can get it," Aunt Gracia said. "Jesus multiplied the fishes to feed the multitude. And that includes you. You're the one who has decided you're Christian. Don't think you're going to start that trick of not eating again, either."

I ate.

Aunt Gracia started making me go to the Friday night services: the rabbi couldn't very well single me out if I wasn't there. But it wasn't her stopping me from going to church on Sundays with Ami. I didn't want to go to church. I didn't want to be reminded of Mary and her baby.

It was a month of Fridays before the rabbi congratulated Mariam and me for doing good in our own courtyards instead of running to Israel where there were already plenty of others planting trees in deserts. We were a credit to our parents who loved us so much, and I was the little Armenian girl who had become part of them.

"He said that on purpose," Aunt Gracia fumed on the way home. "If she's so much a part of them, they wouldn't even remember that she's Armenian."

"What's the difference?" Uncle Samuel said. "It's no secret."

"They don't need to be reminded. It's hard enough finding nice boys nowadays."

That week, I started to wear the silver cross Ami had given me over my blouse, and at school I declared my secret name: "Arta was the first Armenian queen of Jerusalem. She was also the goddess of women and the moon. But you can call me Sosi."

Mariam said she thought I was looking for trouble.

Aunt Gracia put it differently: I was giving her migraine headaches, I was driving her blood pressure up, and I was cutting my own throat. She had heard at the baths that I was using an Armenian name. How long did I think the Behars would put up with this nonsense before they refused to have me? A promise to a best friend was one thing, but ruining your son's life, taking on a mad daughter-in-law was another. And if I thought she was going to call me Sosi after all these years of Zeyneb (how could I dishonour my parents by throwing away the name they had given me) I had another think coming.

She hadn't even noticed my cross.

I cried.


It was spring. The skies were clear. Mariam and I were walking home from the shop with Uncle Samuel. A stork flew in over our heads, extending ungainly legs to land on a rooftop.

The sighting of the first returning stork meant travel, but I would never go anywhere: from my father's home to my husband's to the grave — just like the proverb.

"You'll probably go to Paris for your honeymoon," Mariam said. She sounded envious.

"You can go. I don't want to go to Paris," I said.

"We'll all go," Uncle Samuel said.

"To Paris?" I said.

"Gracia is always blaming me for never taking her anywhere. She's right. I should take her somewhere."

Where she wanted to go was to Istanbul to see the Gracia Mendes Synagogue or Beirut, the Paris of the Mediterranean just down the coast. But he wasn't offering either. No, he was offering Israel which, with returning Jews from all over the world, was being overrun by barbarian Ashkenazis. Israel was never on her wish list.

"Israel?" Aunt Gracia said. "Because you saw a stork you want to go to Israel? They just finished a war there. Five Arab countries are threatening to jump down their throats any minute. What's wrong with Beirut or Istanbul?"

"Chérie, I'm offering you a trip."

"You're up to something, Samuel Reijskind. For forty-five years you can never leave the shop, and suddenly for no reason, you want to take a trip. It's not reasonable."

"Who knows what's reasonable? When I left France, it wasn't reasonable. Then the war came along, and suddenly it was reasonable."

"Why now? Why can't we wait until after the wedding?"

"If Nissim has waited this long, he can wait a few more months. Fifteen isn't too late for her to marry."

A few days later, Mariam and I were walking home from school arguing about the merits of moving. I was voting for the complete unknown. Mariam wasn't interested in the unknown. She preferred familiarity.

Nissim was coming down the street carrying a bundle of clothes to deliver to Aunt Gracia for our collection. He should have been at his factory.

"It's good that you're doing this now, Zeyneb," he said. He was looking proprietary. Like his mother. I could see thoughts of babies dancing in his head. "You won't have time after we're married."

I panicked. "My name's not Zeyneb. It's Sosi Arta. You would be wasting your time marrying me. My babies would die. Armenian babies die. If you don't believe me, you can ask Aunt Gracia. I went to two doctors, and they both say the same thing." I pulled my cross out from under my blouse where I had hidden it because I was almost home and Mariam thought the least I could do was not give Aunt Gracia (her defenceless grandmother) a heart attack. "But probably that's better. If we had children, we'd have to argue about religion. Arguing about religion isn't good for children. Come to think of it, probably the rabbi won't even want to marry us. Father Havonissian would, though, if we promised to bring them up Armenian."

He left. A brown mushroom plumping down the road.

"Zeyneb —" Mariam started.

"Sosi," I said.

"Sosi Arta Zeyneb Gracia Mendes Reijskind," she said. "You lied!"

"I know. My grandfather said anything is worth saving a life, except, of course, killing another life. Do you think it will work?"

"Whose life are you saving?"

"Mine," I said.

But Mrs. Behar still didn't turn up to tell Aunt Gracia that she didn't want me.

The news of our trip to Israel spread and grew. First it was a few weeks, then a few months — then we were moving, all of us, including Maurice and Aimée and Mariam. The Reijskind clan was leaving town. Uncle Samuel heard it first from Father Havonissian.

Aunt Gracia laughed. At the baths (Mariam went and gave faithful reports), she chuckled fondly that her Samuel, a man who hadn't set foot past the market square since the day he had been seduced by a young girl's eyes, this man who had given up his dream of living in Palestine, had looked up and seen a bird, and, suddenly, he thought he could live the life of a bird, free, with no responsibilities, coming down to earth only when he felt like it.

Uncle Samuel had gotten an idea, and the more he thought about his idea, the more he saw that it was good. Armenians had been a part of the landscape of Jerusalem for over a thousand years. Refugees had fled the massacres and found refuge behind the old city walls of the Armenian quarter. Yet they had kept their own daughter in a country which for her would never be anything but a cemetery, and the fact that I was adopted made it even worse — they had been entrusted with my care and had failed me. They had failed themselves. It was obvious, as obvious as the sun, the moon, or a tape measure. They had been measured and found wanting. Father Havonissian was right: the Reijskind clan had no reason to stay. Why should we, Jews and Armenians, die among strangers?

"What are you talking about? Who are these strangers? Armenians were here centuries before the Ottoman Turks came along. My family has been here for five hundred years. You've lived here for almost fifty years. Next you'll be telling me that I'm a stranger, too."

"No. You're still the woman I fell in love with over the soup."

"What would we do there? How would we live?"

"We'll sell silk. Turkey produces the most beautiful silk in the world. If I could start with nothing once, I can do it again. Zaven will look after the shop here. Aisha Hanim will look after the house. You'll have two homes, like royalty."

"He's never been stubborn a day in his life," she announced to the courtyard, "and one day, he sees a stork, and he's a different man."

That night I thanked Mama for my Armenian name, and I thanked Artemis, and I played magnificent volleyball.

The next morning, over breakfast in the courtyard, Uncle Samuel said, "What do you think, Gracia. Should we sell the house?" and Aunt Gracia almost spilled her tea: "I don't recognize you any more. You're crazy. All our married life you've accused me of not being logical — and you? As long as you talk like that, I'm not staying in the same room with you."

That evening, supper had been laid out by Aisha Hanim, and Aunt Gracia had moved into the living room. She was miserable. Uncle Samuel seemed not to notice. He laid out information on the floor beside her about airfares and boat fares, deck class and first class.

I was awakened by the shatter of glass. Aunt Gracia was standing dishevelled and defenceless in the kitchen, a broken teacup at her feet. She hadn't slept. "Now he's talking about selling the house. He might as well tear out my heart as sell my father's house. He's doing it to spite me. What am I going to tell the Behars? She'll ask me. It's a miracle she hasn't asked already. What am I going to say? What will Maurice do in Israel? What will Mariam do? What will any of us do?"

I woke Uncle Samuel. "I'll marry Nissim," I said. "She's too old to leave. You don't want to leave."

"It's not your affair," he said. "This is between Gracia and me. I followed her for the first forty-five years, she can follow me for the next forty. It isn't such a bad deal."

Mariam and I were in the courtyard inking in the destination of our clothes on sugar sack bags. A shipment of cotton was going out to Lebanon and Israel, and our clothes were going with it. Mrs. Behar rustled past in plump mushroom fashion. She didn't wait to be shown in.

"Uh-oh, Zeyneb," Mariam said.

"Sosi," I said.

Aunt Gracia called me in. I could tell from her voice that she was going to have another headache. Mrs. Behar rustled past me with a significant non-proprietary glare. "You see?" Aunt Gracia said. "You've destroyed a friendship. I hope you're happy. You got what you wanted, and this is the last good match I could have made for you. You and Sammy have ruined my life. How can I ever hold my head up again?"

"But aren't I supposed to like him? I don't like him. How am I supposed to have sex with someone I don't like? You like Uncle Samuel."

She blushed.

Mariam and I went to the river. It was clear and fine. Pelicans were back, perched on the bank beside us.

# II

# JERUSALEM

# Chapter 4

We were on our way. The house hadn't been sold: when the next forty years were up, we might want to come back. The Reijskind clan would decide later if they ought to leave: Maurice and Aimée were letting us check out the barbarian level first to determine whether or not it was life threatening. Life in Turkey was peaceful. Israel would be filled with traumatized souls, and Maurice didn't want to expose Aimée and Mariam to all that misery. Ami Zaven was now a seller of both carpets and silk, and Mariam, who had developed a sudden interest in fabric, particularly silk, would help.

Mariam and her mother cried when we left. Aunt Gracia cried. Aisha Hanim wept. Allah would take care of us, she said. "He'd better," Aunt Gracia said.

Maurice looked worried. "My father, the optimist," he said. "Starting a new life at his age."

Uncle Samuel reached up and pinched his cheek: "I'm the same age I've always been. Don't let how I look fool you." He promised we would be back — as soon as the Behars had found a wife for Nissim, and Gracia thought she could go to the baths again.

On the boat, Aunt Gracia plonked herself down in the midst of our suitcases and rolled up carpets. Herring gulls complained, accused, lamented, while the shore, shimmering under the hard sun, drew away from us to become a line on the horizon — and then was gone.

We sat, Aunt Gracia, eyes fixed on where Turkey used to be, Uncle Samuel looking out to sea. The ship rose and fell beneath us on full rolling breaths of blue. We were going deck class. Aunt Gracia refused a cabin. If a ship went down, you drowned first in your first-class cabin. I rolled out our carpets, mine with the blood-red colours of the mountains, Aunt Gracia and Uncle Samuel's with Stars of David in the border. Ami had given it to them. Carpets were currency. You could always sell a carpet.

We fell asleep wrapped in mist. There were no stars.

I awoke to Aunt Gracia's mutterings. "Ha!" she said. "A pool of blood. When have you ever seen a sunrise like that? We'll be lucky if we reach land alive."

The sun had slipped out of a grey satin envelope of sea and sky to spill rose and gold light over the edges, rose petals of light floating on the water, rose petals for the dancing feet of princesses, for sultans' daughters, for Mariam and me. Braziers were set up for coffee, backgammon games were opened. We drifted on a hot and hazy sea. I had wanted Mariam to come with us. She couldn't abandon Aimée and Maurice. She was the only child. She had a duty. "You're off to Armenian land," she said. "I can't follow."

"Are you sure you know your geography?" I said.

"The only person not crying is Father Havonissian," she said. "That should tell you something."

Aunt Gracia spent the day glowering at the rolling breaths of blue.

One lemon mist morning I awoke to see a grey heron perched on the rails, its head tucked between its shoulders and its back turned to us like a crotchety old man. We sighted land, a mirror of the coast we had left behind, waves breaking against a yellow ochre shore, gulls wheeling patterns of white against the sky, white stone houses climbing white stone hills. The anchor splashed into the sea. Heavy ropes were cast to the dock. We formed into lines as the heat and humidity settled and tightened. Uncle Samuel pointed with pride at the Hebrew signs — Israel's fourth anniversary, 5712. Aunt Gracia wasn't impressed. She preferred the comfort of knowing that 1952 in Turkey was 1952 in France was 1952 in... Turkey, for heaven's sake, had a modern calendar. I could read nothing but the numbers. The characters were as foreign as Turkish had once been.

We stood with our bags and boxes and trunks, people swirling around us like sand and disappearing up dusty lanes. Men in black with long ear-locks converged on other men with long ear-locks, the ones on the boat Uncle Samuel had fumed at and argued with about their fundamentalism. One of the pale thin survivors with numbers tattooed on her arm wandered off with nothing but a thin blanket and a half-filled pillowcase. A street vendor appeared with watches. A small boy offered cactus fruit. A woman in a too-big army uniform and delicate gold earrings approached. Her hair was stuffed under an army cap. Everything seemed too big for her, like a stork in argyles. "*Shalom, Guten Tag, bari luis, bonjour... Qu'est-ce que vous-allez? Where do you want to go?*"

"French! She speaks French," Aunt Gracia squealed with relief, spilling out the story of how one day I had decided for no reason that I was Armenian, and now here we were, refugees, vagabonds, looking for a new life with no idea of where we were or what we were doing or how we were going to get there.

"So no one's expecting you," she said. "Except me, a humble cabbie, at your service. Where exactly do you think you want to go?"

"The train station," Uncle Samuel said. "Jerusalem."

"Ah, yes," she said. "Jerusalem. City of a thousand religions and a thousand conflicts. Why didn't you go to Beirut? There are plenty of Armenians there. And nobody is fighting. If I hadn't married Joe, I'd probably be there right now. Well, actually, I wouldn't be there right now. I'd probably be back in Canada."

By the time our luggage was stowed, we knew all about her, that she was Mrs. Varti Gordon (we could call her Varti), a nice Armenian girl married to a nice Jewish boy who had come to the Holy Land for the good of their unborn children. But now he was dead (before she'd had a chance to have those children) and she was still here, and the only thing she got out of it (besides a dead husband) was her parents back in Montreal not speaking to her because she hadn't married an Armenian. (Or her not speaking to them, she wasn't sure which by now.) Never mind the fact that Armenians in Canada were scarcer than hens' teeth.

"So how'd you get to be brought up by Jews? Never mind. It could be worse. My dad was brought up in an orphanage. Shipped him off to Canada to work on a farm. You're in luck, you guys. You've run into the Armenian network first thing — and nothing gets to Armenian heartstrings like an orphan, believe me. You can forget about your hotel idea. Forget the train, too. I'll drive you. If I don't deliver you personally, Meri will never forgive me. Jerusalem is only an hour away, anyway."

We were on a dusty road with sand dunes on one side and sparkling sea on the other. Prickly pear cactus fences held back the sand. Syrian kingfishers with smart blue coats and orange vests perched on fence posts. It was just like home.

"I just called Turkey home," I said.

"What did you expect?" Aunt Gracia said. "You grew up there. People you love died there. Did you think you would bring your whole heart with you?"

"Relax, Sos," Varti said. "You'll fall in love with this place. Take it from me. There's never a dull moment."

"There's nothing wrong with dull moments," Aunt Gracia said. "The world could use a few dull moments." We had just passed a burned-out car. Camels, S's knocked over on their sides, slid along the horizon.

"Bedouins," Aunt Gracia said. "A Bedouin attack."

"Nope," Varti said. "I'm afraid you can't blame the Bedouins. It's a leftover from the '48 war. The Bedouins are peaceful. I'll bet my bottom dollar they'll soon be driving trucks instead of riding camels."

Aunt Gracia was muttering to Uncle Samuel in Turkish: "What are you doing? You don't even know this woman. She could be delivering us to the Bedouins right now. Bedouins have been attacking caravans for centuries. Cars are caravans. All your talk about trust — 'When you travel, you learn who to trust.' If you stay home, you don't have to learn. You know."

Uncle Samuel patted her hand.

"And if I had stayed home, I'd have met a different woman over a different soup."

It was his conversation stopper, that fateful soup.

As we wound up into the Judean mountains, shadows of green, reforestation of pine and cedar, defaced the brilliant light of sky and rock. What trees had been left, mostly on the plains, had been fed to the Hejaz train as it crossed from Damascus in the east to go through Jerusalem and then south to Mecca. The Hejaz train no longer ran through Israel.

Jerusalem was a jumbled city spilling over the spine of the winding Judean mountains. The air was vibrant. The golden walls of limestone rock glowed.

We stopped at an iron gate in front of a two-story stone house, home of Varti's best friend, Meri. They were bonded by widowhood and shared Armenian blood, except that Meri's husband had died of natural causes, and Varti's had been crushed by a tractor. Meri had taken over her husband's photography business after his death, although she had never snapped a picture even once. The house was filled with photographs — of babies, of picnics, of graduations, of weddings, of grandchildren. Of Varti and a young man framed by a frothy snowdrift. Of Varti and the same man on a tractor stuck in sand. They looked sweet. They looked happy.

Aunt Gracia had never allowed photographs. She and Aisha Hanim both believed that photographs stole your soul. Mariam's mother brought out the camera only if Aunt Gracia wasn't around and snatched pictures off the walls if she was coming over. When we were leaving, Aisha Hanim borrowed Mariam's mother's camera: after what she'd gone through with me, she said, she deserved a part of my soul. Aunt Gracia's, too, for that matter.

"Have you ever noticed," Varti said, "that most of the photographers in the Middle East are Armenian? I figure it's because of the genocide. Photographs fool you into thinking you can hang onto the past. 'My whole family may be dead, I may have lost the home place and the vineyard, but dammit, I've still got their pictures.' Once you're up on the wall, you're part of the family, whether you want to be or not. And lucky for us, as long as everyone else is against graven images, we've got the market to ourselves. Zero capital, too. Get yourself a camera, and you're in business."

Varti had settled us with tea and hazelnuts by the time Meri came back from the studio, and had already decided that she would move her base of operations to Jerusalem: after all, Meri was always lobbying for Varti to have more Armenians in her life, and cabs were portable.

Meri took one look at us, my exhausted parents and me, and before Aunt Gracia could begin the apologies for our intrusion, Meri had raised Aunt Gracia's hand to her forehead. We were a blessing. We were welcome for as long as we would stay. If her parents had lived, they would be Aunt

Gracia and Uncle Samuel's age. Who knew if God hadn't guided us to her door?

Meri was speaking to Aunt Gracia in Turkish, and Uncle Samuel in French, and she tried to speak to me in Armenian. She had learned Turkish from the Armenian refugees; she had learned French and English and Arabic in school in the old city; she had learned German because of the German immigrants, and Hebrew because it was the official language.

She had blue eyes. A gentle blue, the blue of faded doors and patience and time.

Our rooms upstairs looked over a garden of olive and pepper trees. Aunt Gracia lay flat on her back, a little round bubble staring up at the ceiling. Uncle Samuel opened the shutters and looked up at the stars. It was still. It was brilliant. Clear. Stars like diamonds. Stars that you could pick and wear in your hair. Mountain stars.

# CHAPTER 5

It was cooling off. Starlings were flying in, roosting on the trees, fluttering, calling, stirring the air with the iridescence of their black feathers. Turtledoves cooed, demure in black lace collars.

And then the cold rains came, and the sparkling days when the city glowed and vibrated in the light and raindrops swelled and glistened on bare branches. Uncle Samuel had colour in his cheeks. He had set up shop with a trunk full of silk that he just happened to have in a spot no one wanted (because it was so close to No Man's Land) but him (because he could see the old city, glowing, unreachable). He had one other neighbour (because it was cheap), Monsieur Abhessara, a Sephardic Jew from Morocco more interested in the rent (none) than in the location. Monsieur Abheserra and his multitude of curly-headed children had swarmed into the shop with brooms and saws and paintbrushes; shelves were up, walls were whitewashed, and the new doors painted an astonishing blue: in the Holy City, men of trade were in particular need of defence against the evil eye. Here when a sole wore out, one did not blame the shoe for walking too many kilometres but the leather which was thin, mangy, cut from worm-eaten hide, and unworthy of serving as a patch for the glove of the most obnoxious of seventh cousins. If a shirt should become too tight, the guilty culprit would be not the expanding stomach but the fabric, woven with silk spun by starved worms which could produce only stingy threads.

Uncle Samuel claimed that he was ready to do battle.

Even Aunt Gracia, furiously knitting hats and mitts and scarves and socks, seemed content. I didn't trust her. I expected eruptions at any moment. "Sweetheart," Uncle Samuel said. "Never underestimate your aunt."

I felt guilty. They were too old to have run away from home.

"We haven't," Uncle Samuel said. "We're only adding rooms. There's nothing wrong with expanding the house. Don't waste time blaming this on God, either. If we credited Him with everything, He'd have a lot to answer for."

Eventually Varti noticed that I was "hanging around the house all day." I should be going to school, planting trees, reading to orphans. Aunt Gracia couldn't see the point: "We'll only be here until Sammy comes to his senses."

"I see," Varti said. "Well, maybe you shouldn't worry about it, Sosi. Something will come up. Life has a way of doing that. Mind you, if you just sit around and let life decide, you can be in trouble. You have to pay attention, too. Maybe, though, being home with Gracia and Samuel keeps you busy enough. They don't seem to have any idea how old they are. Your uncle has got to be seventy-five if he's a day. I have to hand it to him. Imagine what Turkey was like in the 1900s. Or Paris. Imagine leaving Paris. Wow. Who leaves Paris?"

By the time she finished, I was worried about my age, Aunt Gracia and Uncle Samuel's ages, and all our futures, including hers.

In the meantime, Aunt Gracia had been giving me orders. I was learning to cook, to sharpen knives and chop, to feel the weight of a fresh egg, and to look for colour in the gills of a fresh fish. I scoured the markets for the perfect clementines, mandarins, oranges, cactus fruit, mangoes, or grapes; cucumbers, tomatoes, and carrots. With rations of eggs and meat, I excelled at salads and eggplant in disguise: eggplant liver, eggplant chicken, eggplant mushroom... There was something satisfying about being surrounded by all those colours and textures. Maybe I was growing up, Aunt Gracia said. Someday, God willing, I would have a home of my own. If anyone would have me after all the trouble I had caused.

"It wasn't meant to be," I said, borrowing Meri's favourite phrase. In reverse.

"No, I suppose not," Aunt Gracia said. "I guess I should have known better. Sometimes Sam is smarter than I am."

I had been writing regular reports to Mariam and Ami Zaven, and I had a new argument to appeal to Mariam's do-gooder heart to bring her to Jerusalem. I had found Ami's brother. I had studied the photograph of Varti's father, analyzing his amazing eyebrows, his balding head, and his full chubby cheeks. She had to bring him. As soon as Varti saw Ami Zaven she would know that it was true. Ami Zaven would find his brother all because Aunt Gracia tried to marry me off.

Mama would have loved to find one of her sisters.

Varti said I was pipe-dreaming. Or stirring up a hornet's nest. I might consider letting sleeping dogs lie.

"I think it was meant to be," I said.

"There's a fly in the ointment, pipsqueak. I don't remember my father ever talking about a brother. And what's wrong with a plain old picture?"

"Very common among survivors," I said. "Trying to forget painful memories. Besides, pictures aren't the same."

In my next letter to Ami Zaven, I invited him to visit: why not expand the house? His response was that his house was quite big enough for one person, thank you, and someone had to stay home to take care of it.

The next letter was from Aimée. Aimée thought it was a wonderful idea to send Mariam to Jerusalem. She and Aisha Hanim could take care of Zaven's shop, since that seemed to be his major excuse. Mariam was strangely silent.

One morning, Meri wouldn't get out of bed. She wouldn't go down to the studio, and she wouldn't get up; she wouldn't talk to anyone, and she wouldn't eat. The third day, Aunt Gracia sent me in. You never know, Aunt Gracia said, maybe Meri resented having her home taken over, and by Jews at that. "Go ask her if she wants us to leave," Aunt Gracia said. "But be delicate."

I asked her.

Meri glared at me from her pillow.

We had insulted her.

She had gone to school with Baha'i, Greek Orthodox, Abyssinian, Muslim, Jew, Catholic Armenian, and Gregorian Armenian. They had learned each other's languages; they had respected each other's church bells, chants, prayers, and holy days — until the British came along with simultaneous offers of a homeland to the Jews and sovereignty to the Arabs, allowing the Arabs to attack the Jews, and the Jews to counterattack the Arabs, betraying them both and pulling out when they were asked by the United Nations to oversee the peace. Now we, the Armenians, were caught in the middle, of secondary consideration in the old city as well as in the new Israel.

Suddenly she was talking about the genocide. Her husband, Krikor, had spoken of it only once so that she would never ask again. She couldn't blame him — a twelve-year-old boy who had been forced to watch his father being shot was bound to want to forget.

"Krikor's family was probably murdered with the copper from our pots," she said. "Our bullets." She reached into the dresser beside her bed and pulled out a tattered certificate from the Turkish government: an acknowledgement of her family's contribution to the war effort.

Krikor had never blamed them, though. He just wanted to live. While most of the refugees were grateful for the protection of the monastery and happily lived out their lives under the authority of the priests' directives — what they would study, whom they should marry, which apartment they would have — Krikor had refused. By the time he was sixteen he had left to live in the new city. He learned Arabic like an Arab, knew a dozen different routes to Jericho or Galilee by foot, knew which caves provided shelter and which wadis, river courses, held water. With the money he earned as a translator and guide for the British, he bought a camera and was soon selling pictures of the soldiers to send home to parents and sweethearts. By the time he was twenty, she and Krikor were married and had their own photography studio. Then, only a few months before he would have been fifty and their thirtieth anniversary, he was gone.

"All those years, whatever he wanted to do, whatever he said, I never argued with him. He wanted to take me from my family, I agreed. He didn't want me to talk about the massacres with our sons, I didn't open my mouth. The boys moved to Lebanon, I didn't say a word. Now I have nothing." She reached for his picture on the bedside table. "It's been five years, and I still expect him to walk through the door, looking like that. Smiling like that. And every day, I have to go into the shop and create more lies." She smashed it against the bedpost. Caressing eyes lay behind shattered glass.

I ran for Varti. She brought tea. She offered helpful advice that Meri didn't want: it was normal, Varti said, to hate someone after they died. She had been furious at Joe, too, and she wasn't even living on the kibbutz anymore. She had left the unblooming desert to drive the cab in Haifa, and he, rumour had it, had another desert-loving woman.

"You don't understand," Meri said. "We killed his family. The bullets came from our pots."

"The bullets came from your pots because the pots were stolen from you by soldiers with guns. What were you supposed to do?"

"We should have died rather than give them a thing. Now I'm being punished. He's left me alone. Christmas is coming, and I suppose you'll go, too, all of you. It's not bad enough that Krikor and the boys abandoned me."

"I don't have to leave," Varti said. "Taxicabs are portable. And it isn't as if Gracia and Sam have anywhere else to go. They're lucky they made it this far."

The next day, Meri got up. The pre-Christmas fast, the six days without meat or milk, was coming. There were topigs to make, sesame crackers, tahini cookies. Meri and Varti were going into the old city to visit Meri's sister for Christmas, and they wanted to take me along. I was afraid to ask.

"When," Aunt Gracia said, "have I ever objected to anything that was good for you?"

So I was to be allowed to go into the Armenian Quarter for three days over Christmas, the only time of the year Israeli Armenians were allowed into Jordanian Jerusalem. I would be surrounded by Armenians who had never known fear, who walked with the pride of who they were and what they believed, a sea of Armenians who laughed with sunlight in their eyes.

"If that's what you think, kid, you're dead wrong," Varti said. "Half of the Armenian Quarter are old families who have been in Jerusalem since forever, but the other half were refugees from Asia Minor. By the way, I wouldn't use the word 'Turk' or 'Turkish' too often. It's 'Armenian coffee,' and 'Turkey' is 'Asia Minor.' Around here, we still remember that

Asia Minor is under Turkish occupation. A thousand years, mind you, but we remember."

It was cold and clear the morning we were to go in. Aunt Gracia went to bed with a hot water bottle and a headache. "They're going to marry you off," she said dourly. "I've spent almost ten years of my life defending myself for having the gall to bring up one of theirs, and for what? So they can snatch her away right from under my nose."

"Do you want me to stay?" I asked.

"Don't be silly," Uncle Samuel said. "What can happen in three days?"

A lot could happen in three days. Wars could start. Mountains could crack open. People could die.

Uncle Samuel walked with us along the barbed wire corridor through the devastation of No Man's Land to the Mandelbaum Gate. He watched us pass through the shed and climb the side of the valley to the old city. And then we were inside the old city walls, inside the walls of the monastery, walls within walls. I couldn't breathe.

"Hey, Sos," Varti said. "You're among friends."

At mass that night, the chants had the fullness of mountains and open plateaus and hope. Jesus looked down from the icons on the wall, a handsome, dark-haired man with wide, distressed eyes. Papa's eyes. A procession of Jesuses with Papa's eyes. Papa's Turkish eyes. The patriarch swept in, his purple brocade robes shimmering in the silken lamplight, emeralds and rubies flashing in the mitre in his hand. Father Havonissian would be saying mass tonight, too, in a simple black cassock, trying to forget the bare walls, the cracks, the leaking roof. I looked again at the satin and the jewels, at Jesus in his gold-leaf halos, at the congregation, whispering, gossiping, as though this were something that happened every day — and I was an *odar*, a stranger.

The next morning, I awoke to Meri and her sister Arpi arguing in ordinary, everyday Armenian, but too quickly for me to understand. I poked Varti. She rolled over and yawned and translated. "Oh, that," she said. "Same old thing. Arpi is still mad at Meri for marrying a refugee instead of a local. She's never forgiven Krikor for taking Meri away."

"But that was over thirty years ago," I said.

"Who said emotions were logical?" Varti said.

"I don't belong here," I said. "I'm going home."

"You can't. We're let in and out on designated days. You're lucky we're not staying with any of the refugees still living in the monastery. They have a curfew, lock the gates. You can't even get to the rest of the old city. Relax. You're just a kid, for Pete's sake. What's life going to be like if you can't even relax when you're a kid?"

We got up. I was going to relax if it killed her.

"Where are we going?"

"To church."

We had just gone to church. It hadn't relaxed me. I hadn't thought she was that religious, either.

"I'm not," she said. "Being religious has nothing to do with it. For me, being Armenian is like skin. You can't take it off. I know. I've tried. The older I get, though, the more I want to be with people who know who I am. Besides, if you're not proud of yourself, kid, no one is going to do it for you. I'm proud of us. I'm proud of our history. Armenians have been leaving footprints on these cobblestones" — we were leaving footprints on the cobblestones — "for more than a thousand years. Mind you, around here a thousand years might not mean anything, but where I come from, anything over a hundred years is a big deal. You gotta be positive, kid. Make things a big deal."

I made things a big deal. The church, richly patterned carpets underfoot, walls and pillars of marble, rosewood, tortoiseshell, mother-of-pearl — every object, every inch inlaid, painted, carved, embroidered, filigreed — was worthy

of an Armenian queen. I tried to imagine Mama standing here,
leaving her footprints on a thousand years of history. The
history she had known nothing of.

She should have been born in Jerusalem.

She would be alive.

She would have wanted to live.

"Don't look now," Varti said, "but I think someone has
his eye on you."

I had seen him the night before. I had thought it was
my imagination. Boys never looked at me. Even Nissim hadn't
really looked at me.

He had intense black eyes, and perfectly arched
eyebrows, and a full delicious mouth.

"Cute, isn't he?" Varti said.

"No," I said.

"Go on," she said. "You're blushing."

When we left, he was right behind us. His name was
Ara. I loved his name. I loved his mouth. He was staring. I
looked down at the damp cobblestones. Our footprints melted
while he stared and Varti told him that I was living proof that
not all Turks were bad. He didn't want to talk about Turks, at
least not about Turks who weren't all bad. He wanted to talk
about art. Aimée had talked about art. Paris was full of art,
she said. Europe was the centre of the artistic world. The
Middle East, with the interdiction against representation, was
in the Dark Ages. Worse.

"What kind of art?" I asked.

"Modern," he said. There was an art show from Soviet
Armenia, and for once it wasn't about tractors and fat-cheeked
children. For once, this art show, unlike others that had come,
was a true expression of the Armenian spirit. It was hard to
believe that the Soviet Armenian government had allowed
these paintings out. Of course, the artists still could have been
banished to Siberia.

The catch was that the exhibit was at the AGBU, the Armenian General Benevolent Union, which was pro-Soviet. Ara was a Dashnak, which was anti-Soviet. Normally, a Dashnak wouldn't set foot in the AGBU because it expressed support for the Soviets in Armenia, and the more support the Soviets had, the longer it would take to get them out. If Arpi, like Ara, a Dashnak and therefore anti-Soviet, found out that we had visited the enemy camp, she would never forgive us. Varti, though, was unprincipled. As long as it was Armenian, it was good enough for her. Besides, she said, all this Dashnak/AGBU stuff gave her a headache: she could never remember who was on which side. Half the time, she couldn't remember which group was supposed to be anti-Soviet, and which pro-Soviet. Her parents hadn't cared; they had simply scraped together whatever they could to send to Armenia.

I had thought everybody was against the Soviets. Nobody wanted them in Armenia. Everyone knew it was a ploy to get as close to the Turkish border as possible. On Uncle Samuel's radio, reports of starvation and oppression in Armenia had been continuous. When Ami Zaven talked about where he would go, he didn't talk about going to Soviet Armenia.

Ara was listening. I blushed. Varti introduced me, new arrival from Asia Minor.

"I knew it," he said. "Of course. Anyone from Asia Minor would be anti-Soviet. They know the truth." He congratulated me on my escape: he couldn't imagine living day in, day out, with murderers, never free of the people who had stolen our lands and murdered our grandparents.

" — Uh," Varti said. "Maybe we could talk about something else? This is Christmas, remember? Season of hope?"

The club was alight with girls in flared skirts and bright wool sweaters and boys with slicked-back hair flitting around each other. A record was on, an Armenian love song, a song of longing. A procession of paintings lined the walls, gentle blues and yellows with the clear light of the mountains.

One of the slicked-back-hair boys came up to Ara: "I guess this means you'll have to admit there is freedom of expression in Armenia, after all?"

"Sure, if you'll admit that Armenians are being sent to Siberia and that Armenian farms are being robbed to feed Moscow."

I had heard the same arguments in our cracked and falling-down church or over tea in Ami Zaven's shop. Always there was the same conclusion: Soviet Armenia was the first Armenia in 500 years, and it mustn't be allowed to fail. It didn't matter that the reason the Armenian Republic had been established — to assuage the guilt of the Allies after World War I for having done nothing to stop the genocide — was wrong. It didn't matter that the Armenian Republic had been betrayed only two years later when Turkey threatened takeover in 1920 and the allies "suggested" that Armenia should accept Russia's offer of "protection." None of that mattered. The continued existence of the country mattered.

"Now there's a passionate young man with a lot of opinions," Varti said as soon as the door closed behind us. "If I didn't think your aunt would drop dead on the spot, I'd tell you to go for him."

"He's a lot like my grandfather," I said. "The Turkish one."

"No one has to know which one," she said. "Keep it for the grandchildren."

Varti extolled his virtues all the way home: tall (for an Armenian and compared to me), dark (weren't we all?), handsome, talented, and twenty. He and his older brother had been trapped in the old city during the war that broke out in '48 when the formation of the state of Israel was approved: Israel had decided that the Armenians who were caught in Jordanian Jerusalem were traitors. The rumour was that the priests were planning to send him to study engineering at the American University in Beirut. He could go to Beirut, but he couldn't go home to Jaffa. His parents had a photography studio there. They would move to Beirut to be with Ara. After their older son was killed in the crossfire of the war, they had no intention of losing the second one.

"You're lucky, you know," Varti said. "You'll never get the flak I got for marrying Joe. No matter who you marry, Armenian, Muslim, or Jew, somebody's going to be happy about it."

"And unhappy," I said. "Mariam's mother says that with Aunt Gracia and Aisha Hanim and Father Havonissian each representing one of the world's great religions, I'll ruin somebody's life no matter what."

Each time I had refused to bow to Mecca or say the Islamic prayers, each time I had gone to the synagogue with Aunt Gracia or to church with Ami Zaven, Aisha Hanim had bewailed my betrayal of my Turkish blood. And each time she had said it, I thought of Emek and of the children in my village, of Mama and Papa dead, blue flower eyes and blood and bone scattered over the plain.

And then I would think of my grandfather, my loving, laughing grandfather.

"Everybody's always telling me what I am, and who I shouldn't betray, and who I shouldn't marry or who I should," I said.

"Relax, Sos," Varti said. "I didn't want to get married when I was fifteen, either. Eighteen is a different story, though, take it from me. Sex, you know. You can't get away from it. How many people would get married — I mean, people whose parents don't marry them off — if it weren't for sex?"

No one had ever talked to me about sex before, not Aunt Gracia when she was marrying me off, not Mariam whose every waking thought was of babies. Even Mariam's mother never got past the mechanics of "a woman's time."

"Darn," Varti said. "I could use some right now. Sex, that is."

Arpi and Meri were still fighting. We could hear them as we ascended the spiral staircase to the third floor. Now, though, it was about Varti and me. Arpi would never be able to lift her head again; her reputation in the community was ruined: Meri had allowed Varti and me, guests in her home, to enter the AGBU, the spawning ground of traitors.

"Wow," Varti said. "News travels fast."

"That's exactly why Krikor and I left," Meri announced in a fury. "You can't make a move here without everyone knowing about it — who you visit and who you don't, what you bring and what you're wearing, what you say and when you leave. Half of the community isn't speaking to the other half, but everyone knows everything about everyone else all the time. Forty years later, refugees from Asia Minor are still 'refugees,' their children are 'refugees,' and their children's children will probably be refugees. Armenians can't even get along with each other, yet we expect everyone else to care about what happens to us. I'll go to that art show myself. I don't care if you come or not."

"You were never like this before you married Krikor," Arpi shouted after her. "You used to be reasonable."

Arpi sat glaring at the red geranium on her windowsill. Varti and I set out lunch in front of her — bean salad, hummus, pita bread, olives. She took an olive. When Meri came back an hour later, Arpi was still glowering. Meri was glowing: The art show had been uplifting. The artist had been orphaned at the age of three and lived on the streets, yet with all he had suffered, he painted such joy, while she and Arpi couldn't even get along on the one day of the year that is about love. "Isn't that why Jesus was born?" she said. "To bring the message of love?"

"I can't help it," Arpi said. "I wait all year for you, and..."

"Yup," Varti said. "Right on schedule. Time to clear the decks. This is when somebody cries."

We left. As we passed the monastery, a monk in an earth brown habit looked up from his book and pointed at a clock: the gates closed at 7:00.

"No wonder Krikor left," Varti said. " It's like having a babysitter. You never get to grow up. And he looks so cute in his little brown hood, too. I hope he's not going to be one of the celibate ones. It's such a waste."

We turned into the Arab quarter, down narrow cobbled stairs to an underground souk. The aroma of cardamom and olives, leather and coffee filled the air. Narrow shops lined the streets: shoemakers, tinsmiths, spice vendors, candle makers, butcher shops, teashops... Women, patient, weathered, in black robes with vibrant red embroidery, squatted beside strings of garlic and bundles of dried herbs. We moved over for a camel. Cats lay on the roofline, waiting. A butcher threw them scraps.

Ara was there.

He offered us each a pastry. He watched as I bit into a sticky honey-soaked *lokhma*. I stopped chewing. He bit into a *lokhma*. Varti disappeared.

"I saw you in a dream," he said. "I saw your eyes."

"I don't think so," I said.

"Yes," he said.

He walked me back to Arpi's telling me about his dream: he had been waiting for me all his life. The fact that I'd had such a weird history only made me more endearing, more in need of protection. Restoration.

Varti was sitting in the window beside the geranium. "Ah, romance!" she said. "I'm jealous. Romance is so wonderful. Of course, this could be a tragedy, and not a romance at all. You're lucky you won't be here long enough to really fall for him. As long as Israel won't let the Armenians who were caught here in the '48 war back in, you'll be separated by a wall."

In bed that night, I thought of paintings of blue and yellow light. I thought of Ara's eyes. I thought of his mouth. Next Christmas felt very far away. We could be back home in Turkey by then. I would forget what he looked like, his mouth, his dark intense eyes, his thick eyelashes.

I hid my head under the covers.

There was snow the next morning, a thin snow on cobbled streets. We would leave as soon as Meri had finished a shoot. It was to be a group family portrait. There were three grandparents, five children, eleven grandchildren, and three great-grandchildren. I tilted hats, placed hands, sat children on knees, arranging a family to be held by time. When the children wanted to know whose curly hair they had or whose pursed mouth, whose genius for drawing or whose bad humour, they would have an answer.

And then we were ready to go, standing at the gates, the breath of hundreds frosting in the shadows of the old city walls.

"Speak of the devil," Varti said.

Ara sauntered over and put his arm around my shoulder as though it belonged there. I felt like it belonged there. I wanted it there. He was shivering. He had been wearing a coat the last time I had seen him, a navy woollen coat with a white scarf that was delicious against his dark hair and eyes. "What are you doing here?" I asked. "What happened to your coat?"

He looked at me intently. "It's amazing. You're as sweet as I remembered." He shivered again. "The way the Arabs and Jews get along has nothing to do with us," he said. Loudly.

"We should be able to come in whenever we want. Any time of year. Any holiday."

Twelve people turned to hiss at him.

When our papers were checked, Ara was no longer Ara Mamoulian, but Berj Davidian.

"Who's Berj Davidian?" I said.

"A figment of my and my forger's imagination inspired by the gift of a coat. Berj. Happy. Happy Son of David. Good choice, don't you think? I don't know why I didn't think of this before. I could have been home years ago — if I hadn't had to wait for you."

"You're crazy," I said.

And then, as we stood under the frosty sun he started to tell me about his father's garden — mangoes and avocado, oranges and grapefruit, lemons, banana, and breadfruit; warblers and crows and kingfishers and starlings all celebrating life in his father's garden.

We were out. Off the path, in among the weeds and grass still green under lace snow scarves, a tit perched on the sturdy seeds of a globe thistle and tugged. Uncle Samuel was standing at the bottom of the hill in a halo of bright diamond snow. I ran down the long slope. Ara bowed over Uncle Samuel's hand: he wished to honour the man who had saved my life, the man who had staved off the Turkish dogs.

I remembered my father holding Mama in the night, calming her out of her nightmare. I remembered my grandfather railing at the ungodly ways of men.

"I'm half Turkish," I said.

"In blood, maybe. Not in your soul."

"What do you know about my soul?"

"What's going on?" Uncle Samuel said.

"Nothing," I said.

I watched Ara leave.

At her gate, Meri stood and breathed in the greenery. Frost had melted off the trees. She smiled at her garden. Our dusty hooded crow, his black head and tawny coat looking newly washed and pressed, cawed.

Aunt Gracia was waiting in a chair beside the bedroom window wrapped in a shawl and blanket. She beamed from her cocoon, little and cute without her teeth. "You caught me without my teeth," she said. "I wanted to look pretty for you."

I cried. I hugged her and I cried.

# CHAPTER 6

"Cripes," Varti said. "You've got this swell guy after you. What are you moping around for?"

"I'm not moping." A letter from Ara in Jaffa was being delivered every day to Meri's studio. "'Blue eyes waiting for laughter, remember?' Would you answer someone who said he saw you in a dream?"

"It can't hurt to answer a letter," she said. "Don't you want some fun in your life?"

"Fun?" I said.

It was a new concept. What was fun? Even playing with Mariam when I was small hadn't really been "fun," not with, as Aunt Gracia put it, all that killing and dying, and volleyball was more like a combat zone.

From Meri, I received a lecture about the crusaders and why she and I had a right to be proud of our blue eyes. They were a badge of honour indicating both a people who gave shelter (us, the Armenians) and a people who spread truth (the crusaders). Aunt Gracia had never had anything good to say about the crusaders, rampaging Christians raping and pillaging their way across Asia Minor and the Middle East in the name of their Saviour.

"Rape, you mean?" I said to Meri. "Did they rape Armenians, too? But we're Christian. Why would they rape us?"

"They didn't. They married us. Armenian women have always been beautiful. There are plenty of other blue-eyed Armenians. If you don't want him, he'll find someone else."

I didn't feel better.

"I should never have agreed to bring you," Aunt Gracia said. "At least at home you were going to school."

"You didn't want me to go to school. You wanted me to get married."

"Don't remind me," she said. "Look at you. You used to be a healthy girl, now you sit around the house worrying about boys."

"I'm not worrying about boys," I said. "And I'm not sitting around. I'm helping at the studio." So far, helping meant sitting on a stool behind the counter waiting for someone to come in to make an appointment or pick up photographs. Occasionally, I filled the developing pans and hung photographs up to dry.

That night in my dream I was standing in the Armenian cathedral. Jesus, sad, in spite of his gold-leaf halos, was watching me. The silver filigree oil lamps gleamed. I was being married to Nissim. I awoke just in time to save myself.

Varti was in the kitchen reading an Armenian newspaper smuggled in from Jordan, a gift from a politician (a woman, no less, who left her husband and children at home) she had driven to a meeting on the Jordanian border. These clandestine night meetings between Jews and Arabs were probably the only ones that would succeed. Because of the silence and the stars. Because of the knowledge of what we shared, and how little we mattered. She fantasized sometimes that she would meet an Armenian/Arab cousin. On the kibbutz, even though she had been afraid of Arab attacks, she had always wanted the chance to shout out, "Are you Armenian?" The survivors of the genocide spoke of the Arabs with gratitude and respect. During the marches, almost the only source of food or *labban* was when they passed an Arab encampment. The Arabs sold as much food as they were able under the eye of the Turkish guards. Sometimes they agreed to take in a child. When they could do nothing, at least there was pity in their eyes rather than avarice or loathing or lust.

I told her my dream.

"Your dreams," Varti said, "are not your friends. Why can't you just have sexy dreams like I do? Mind you, I wish I didn't. No wonder they married kids off at the age of thirteen. All those jumping hormones.

"Tell you what. You're going to learn to drive. There's nothing like going too fast around tight corners. Of course, being shot at is good, too. Did you know that there are actually people who find torture and killing sexy?"

"No," I said.

"Yeah, well, you don't need to know that. Makes you lose faith in human nature."

I was a good driver. A fast learner. Quick reflexes. An instinct for walls and the chickens or children who jumped out from behind them. I could see in the dark, the heritage of four thousand years of shepherding under the light of the stars, according to Varti: in no time at all, I would know Jerusalem like the back of my hand.

I wrote to tell Ara about my driving. He said women didn't need to know how to drive, especially if they were getting married.

"Wow, so young and already an old-world jerk."

"Don't you like him any more? Aren't I supposed to like him?"

"You can like him, just keep an eye on him. Joe was never like that."

She took me for test runs. She taught me her patter and her routes. The Christian tour was necessarily skimpy because most of the sites — the Mount of Olives, the Garden of Gethsemane, the Via Dolorosa, Bethlehem, the Church of the Nativity — were in Jordanian Jerusalem or the West Bank. The old city walls glowed, unapproachable, like God, in the distance.

A smart guide gave them what they wanted. That Jesus' manger was actually a cave, and a cave that had previously been a sanctuary dedicated to Jupiter and Adonis, was either interesting or blasphemous. You didn't pass it on to everyone. Pilgrims didn't come to the Holy Land to learn that. Ditto the information that the "holy" glow had nothing to do with God, that it was simply the colour of the limestone rock. Or that living in the Holy City had almost always been closer to living in hell rather than heaven except during the time of Kings Solomon and David when there had been a water system and bathing pools, and the Roman period with their ubiquitous aqueducts, reservoirs, and underground pipes. After the Romans left, the water system went to rack and ruin. Water depended on what you could catch, and since it never rained at all from May to October, how much could you catch? When immigrants started coming in the mid 1800s, they had taken one look at the narrow winding alleys and the open sewers, held their noses and started building outside the old city walls. It was only when the British took over from the Turks after World War I and set up a system to pipe in fresh water that the old city became liveable. Of course, the water system wasn't a heck of a lot better than what the Turks had at home, and we had to admit that Suleiman the Magnificent was the one who had put in place most of what we were romantic about in the old city, the old city walls, the ramparts, the gates. That limestone golden glow.

Some sites were hits with almost everyone. The Russian compound, for instance. Almost everyone hated Russia, either because they had suffered under the Czars, or because they hated Communism. During the 1920s, as many as 20,000 ragged Russian pilgrims had lined up for their supper of an onion and a slice of bread under the shadow of the onion-domed church. Of course, if my client happened to be Armenian, I had to first determine how she/he felt about Russia controlling Armenia. If they were pro-Russian, I might wish to point out that Russia had erected the barracks and church during the Crimean War specifically for the pilgrims, and that an onion and a slice of black bread during the '20s when Russia was rebuilding after the revolution was a respectable meal. No matter what, though, if I ever did get an Armenian client, I was to play up my Armenian blood, living proof that through waves of domination by the Persians, the Greeks, the Romans, the Seljuks, and the Ottomans, we Armenians had been the one constant.

We took Aunt Gracia and Uncle Samuel and Meri so I could practise. Meri already knew everything I knew and could add. Aunt Gracia and Uncle Samuel nodded agreeably no matter how much I did or didn't play up my Armenian blood. We drove to the sea. Aunt Gracia was beginning to concede that travelling wasn't so bad after all, although she didn't see an awful lot of difference between this coast and the Turkish coast. In fact, if the only thing that travelling had to teach her was that most of the world was the same, she might as well have stayed home.

She was homesick. "Don't tell Sammy," she said.

But he knew. I wrote to Mariam. There wasn't a moment to lose. If she didn't bring Ami Zaven soon, we would be back in Turkey, and he would have missed out on a brother.

Varti's car wasn't back one morning. The second morning, Aunt Gracia produced a Bedouin theory. Meri sent a message to Haifa to the family Varti had boarded with. They hadn't heard from her in months. By now, I knew who the best source would be — another cabbie. Cab drivers, according to Varti, were the hawks and owls of a city, an unofficial secret service. Cab drivers knew who came and when they went. They knew policemen and thieves, husbands and lovers. They knew where to get prostitutes, alcohol, and contraband ham. They knew which priests and pious men of all three of the world's great religions bought them and for how much.

I stopped a cab in the street in front of Meri's studio.

"Yeah," the driver said. He was a short tired man who needed a shave. His car looked just like Varti's, round, green, and hunched. "She's in the hospital. I told her. We all told her. This is no job for a woman. She picks up a couple of guys. They jump her. They take her car. She'd rather lose her foot than that car."

He drove us to a hospital. We walked through broad hallways past nurses in white uniforms and starched caps.

"Well, it's about time somebody showed up to spring me," Varti said. She had a cast on her arm. Her good arm. The driving arm. She was in a white hospital gown. "All this white is getting to me. It's like living in negative. Pretty soon I'm going to think I'm in someone's photo file. Or that I'm dead. You should have brought your camera, pipsqueak. Photos Of The Dead. The beginning of your career."

Meri didn't like jokes about death.

"So what happened to you?"

"Nothing," Varti said. "It was my fault. I forgot my own advice — don't fight back when someone rapes you or steals your car. Especially if you're outnumbered. If I hadn't tried to beat them up with Joe's baseball bat, they would have just taken the car. But I made them mad. They did drop me off at the hospital, though. They were embarrassed. Beating up on a girl doesn't give you many points, even if she does have a baseball bat. Serves them right."

We "sprung" her, and she starting wandering the streets looking for her car — any excuse to be out of the house was a good excuse. She spotted it on her way back from the market one day, but how do you follow a car when you're on foot? The car looked unhappy, she said, like it wanted to come home and have a bath: "That's it," she said. "That car is going to be back in twenty-four hours, or he's a dead man."

"Who's 'he'? And who's going to kill him?" Meri said. "You? With your good arm?"

"I have friends," she said. "We know everyone, remember? If I can't get a posse out of them, at least I'll get information."

Meri offered to teach Varti photography while she was waiting for the fear of death to work its magic, but Varti wasn't ready for a darkroom. She took up Aunt Gracia's offer of keeping eye on Uncle Samuel at the shop instead. Aunt Gracia was worried about him. She was writing to Maurice, hoping that someone would come and take them home. Maurice was writing to Uncle Samuel, and Uncle Samuel was writing back that there was nothing to worry about: "You know what your mother is like." Varti was heaping blankets on him, making tea, and haranguing passers-by in Armenian, French, English, bad Arabic, worse Hebrew, and terrible Yiddish. There weren't enough passers-by, not for silk, at least. Most of the passers-by were for Mr. Abhessera. Silk was a luxury. Shoes were a necessity. Not only that, Uncle Samuel seemed to give away more than he sold, although he claimed that there was no such thing as "giving stuff away": there was balance and trade in life.

She arrived home with a length of poppy red silk. She was embarrassed. "He outfoxed me," she said. "All that stuff about bringing out the red lights in my hair."

Meri confiscated it and made it into a blouse. Meri and Aunt Gracia had been plotting since they first learned of Varti's bloody and unsalvageable army uniform. Maybe now she would come to her senses — work with Meri in the studio, take over the studio; meet a nice Armenian man, marry a nice Armenian man. But Varti had a second uniform, and all of Joe's kibbutz work clothes as well, sturdy army grade shorts and pants and shirts. With the olive green of Joe's pants, with her vibrant hair and olive skin, the poppy red was strikingly sensuous.

"You're beautiful," Meri said. "You should get married and have children."

"Not me," Varti said. "Once kids latch onto you with their tiny hearts, they never let go. You're finished. People walk over glass and jump off cliffs for their kids. Not me, forget it."

"It's not so bad," Aunt Gracia said. "There's no greater gift than the trust of a child."

"Yeah, well, from what I hear, they're not all so trusting," she said.

She put the blouse away. It was giving everyone the wrong idea.

Ami Zaven wrote. Mariam had told him about his "brother." He had finally been forced to admit that he had been living for the dream of a brother. Who knew if he even had a brother, if he hadn't constructed this brother along with imaginings of sweaters and breakfast? He should have left with the others, gone to California, to Lebanon, Syria, Venezuela, England, France — anywhere. Instead, he had waited, and for what? To die? When he had had so many opportunities to do that as a child?

He had finally been forced to admit that his life had been futile.

Uncle Samuel glared at me. "Who told you to mix in?"

"Why are you mad at me? Mariam told him. I didn't."

"For heaven's sake," Aunt Gracia said. "It doesn't matter if they're brothers or not. They both need one. I wouldn't be surprised if Zaven is Varti's uncle. They're exactly alike."

"Hey," Varti said. "How did I get into this?"

"You're both afraid to be disappointed. Otherwise you would have written to your parents."

"Why should I write to my parents? So they can be happy Joe's dead? Leave me out of it. I didn't invent this uncle." She slammed out of the house.

I was to write to Ami Zaven to apologize, and Mariam and I were to give up establishing identities and creating brothers: there was as much chance of two bald men who had been separated at five and three being brothers as there was of any of Uncle Samuel's brothers and sisters emerging from their mass graves.

The only thing "the word" turned up was where the car was kept: somewhere in the maze of twisting lanes and tired wooden houses near the Russian Compound. The hunt was on, and I was part of the posse. This was playing infidels and curs for real.

We set out at midnight. A duck quacked. A cat yowled. There was no moon. We didn't take a flashlight. We didn't want anything to see us before we saw it. "You thief, you worm, you slimy despicable bug," Varti shouted into the night. "You deserve to be fed to the hyenas, to be tied to a stake under the desert sun and boiled in oil. You've stolen from the wrong guy this time. If that car isn't back in twenty-four hours, every cab driver in the country will be after you with shovels and axes and hoes. And bring it back clean, dammit, the way you found it."

The next morning the car was back. I looked out of the window, and there it was, hunched, green, and shiny like a patient, friendly frog. Varti was hugging it.

"Varti," I said. "If everything is meant to be, what was the 'meant to be' in all of this? I mean, why would God want you to get cut up and bloody for nothing? The car is back, the guys who beat you up are who knows where..."

"And I'm wearing a blouse and Meri thinks she can marry me off. Don't ask me philosophical questions," she said.

Varti wasn't ready to get back in the saddle. She was a coward simply because she now understood that she could be hurt and die. One would think that her own mortality wouldn't be such a surprise: "Sosi, something terrible has happened to me. I can't make myself get back out on the road. I drive up to the hotel to wait for a fare, and the car just turns itself around and comes right back home. Maybe the guys were right. Maybe it is no job for a woman. A man would climb right back up on the horse. I can't get back up on the horse. I think I've been giving you the wrong advice. Grab life while you can, Sos. If that kid Ara wants to marry you, go for it."

"He can't marry me. He said he doesn't believe in mixed marriages. I'm mixed. Turkish and Armenian. Cur and infidel."

"Not in his eyes, you aren't," she said. "I know how his mind works. There's enough death and destruction in your background to qualify you as a purebred. Besides, unless you marry yourself, all marriages are mixed."

I reported to Ara that all marriages were mixed. He said to go ahead and do the Turks' job for them: the dearest wish of every Turk was that the last Armenian would disappear from the face of the earth. If I wished to aid in the destruction of my own people by marrying a non-Armenian, a mixed marriage (absorption, assimilation) was the quickest way to do it. Next to mass murder, that is.

And speaking of Varti, he added, she had had a mixed marriage, and it hadn't lasted.

"What a swell guy," Varti said. "I can't believe it. So young and already so self-righteous. Maybe he's not as nice as I thought. He doesn't deserve you. I was going to drive you to Jaffa to see him, but he can forget it. I guess we could go to Tel Aviv instead — see a movie, sit in a café, look at the sea. But that's too much like fun. We'll go to the Dead Sea instead. There are monasteries about a thousand years old carved in rock smack in the middle of the desert. It's enough to turn you into a monk on the spot."

We started off in the morning with frost on our breath, wound over and down through the Judean hills. The temperature rose. The sky opened up. The winter rains had brought the wadis, the seasonal riverbeds, to life with finches and storks, hawks and ducks, active lizards and nervous bugs, diminutive deer and bright spring flowers.

The Dead Sea was ghostly. The water was flat, without a ripple, without a duck or frog or water reed, just a salt-encrusted shore and cracked red earth framing empty mirror blue. Salt crystal formations glittered in the sun. Rock cliffs, a shimmering curtain of mauve, towered in the west.

The kibbutz was a camp of huts and tents and scratching chickens and ploughed fields. A tractor was ploughing the earth. I'd never seen one before. In the mountains, the women had done everything by hand, the turning of the soil, the sowing of seeds, the cutting and winnowing. Papa and Mama always worked together: he said a djinni had brought her, and if he didn't keep an eye on her, a djinni might spirit her away. I used to be afraid that a djinni would take me, too: he said it couldn't. Half of me was him. I belonged to the earth.

We came to a stop in a cloud of red earth dust. Chickens scattered. A statuesque woman with a long blond braid dropped a shovel and strode over to envelop Varti in a hug.

"She's back," someone muttered. "Another mouth to feed."

"Right," Varti said. "I'd almost forgotten why I left."

"Don't pay any attention. We're all tired," Freda said. She went back for her shovel and dragged it in the earth behind her. "We need a holiday."

"You'll have to have meetings for the rest of your life before that happens. 'Is it in the ideology?' 'can the kibbutz spare you?' 'shouldn't the oldest member go first?' 'shouldn't the children be considered first?'..."

They both laughed. Hysterically. "It's Joe's anniversary, isn't it?" Freda said. "That's why you're here. You didn't come here to make yourself miserable just for the fun of it."

"Yup." Varti pulled a bottle of Scotch out of her duffle bag, a consolation prize from one of the cab drivers for losing her car instead of a foot. "It's my annual how-guilty-can-I-feel-today trip. I think I actually believe that if I hadn't agreed to emigrate, he wouldn't have come, and he wouldn't be dead. Or maybe I believe that if I hadn't left him, the tractor wouldn't have flipped."

Freda lived like a monk, in a cramped one-room cabin, bare, with a trunk, a bed, three hooks on the wall, and a wash basin: "Sure you don't want to come back?" she said.

"Not unless you can guarantee that I won't have any more of those dreams about jellybean hot water bottles."

She would spend the day watering potato plants, and then she dreamt about them, full bushy plants that she watered and watered, but when she pulled them up, there were no potatoes, just hot water bottles, pink ones and blue ones and red ones and green ones, piles and piles of jelly bean hot water bottles. She would wake up hungry and cold and write home to her parents for another hot water bottle. In the morning, she tore the letter up because if there was any fuel or water to spare (water that didn't eat rubber, that is) neither would go to a hot water bottle.

"Ah, yes," Freda said, "so much to worry about and so little time." Planting a potato was fraught with danger: will the seed potatoes last through the winter? will the seed potato seed? will the seed potato grow?... They could have chosen Safed, an ancient city with a spectacular view of the Hula plains — high, cool, rainy, and out of reach of the swamp mosquitoes below. Or the Sea of Galilee with its gentle grassy shores, its drinking water, and its multitude of little fishes. But no. A bunch of Jews had moved to Israel to be farmers, and there wasn't one farmer or gardener among them, every last one of them children of peddlers or tailors. At least Varti had farming blood. Leave an Armenian on a desert, and in three weeks, you had fresh tomato and parsley sandwiches. In two years, you had olive oil and wine.

"Are you sleeping with anybody?" Varti asked.

"Not anyone who can stay the night," Freda said. "The last thing I thought was that I was going to be cold in the Holy Land."

"If you guys weren't such snobs and read the New Testament, you'd have known that," Varti said. "Why do you think Joseph wanted to find an inn? Well, a cave, actually. He found a cave. By the way, you're raving. Go home, Freda. Meet a nice Jewish boy with no garden and settle down."

And they both laughed again. Hysterically. They were citizens of the world. They didn't fit in anywhere. Here they were, they said, living it up in the Holy Land.

Varti picked up her whiskey bottle. The sun was setting. We were off to Joe's grave. Joe had a thing about desert sunsets, always going on about colours she couldn't see. Freda excused herself. Communing with ghosts wasn't her thing.

"Don't worry," Varti said. "No ghost of Joe there. Joe always knew where he was. It was part of his charm. This is purely a sentimental journey."

The moon was full. The sea was a sheet of silver. The cliffs in the distance were a curtain of silver and black. A chicken clucked. There were no mosquitoes. There was nothing for a mosquito to live on at the Dead Sea. Varti opened the bottle of whiskey and toasted the moon. "Did you know, pipsqueak, that deserts are the most popular place for the gods? Jehovah, Jesus, Allah, Mohammed, they're all here. On this desert. All of us using the same Book. And fighting about it. Can you believe it? Or maybe we just look for excuses to fight, no excuse too small. Personally, I'd worship a tree. Go back to nature. I mean, look at this place. Don't you think a few trees would come in handy? Shade, wood, birdies, bees, a little pot of honey. And fish. Jesus had the right idea about those little fishes. I wouldn't mind a grilled fish this minute. No fish in this sea. What a place. What are we doing here? Do you know that there are at least eleven new Jimmy Stewart movies — what a sweet guy — since we came and I haven't seen any of them? Why aren't there more guys like him?"

"Who's Jimmy Stewart?" I said.

I reached for the bottle. She slapped my hand away.

"Nope. Too young. We're having a serious discussion. There's God, wiping out one tribe after another. 'Don't like me? Gone.' 'Like me — take a seat.' Petty, or what? And the things that He allows to go on. Lot's daughters get him drunk so he'll have sex with them — incest, we're talking incest, here, group incest — talk about desperate, sex-starved women. I mean, really. They'd lock him up today. Then Jesus comes along, and what happens? He dies. Painfully, too. To save us. What kind of lesson of the purpose of life is that? I'd go for Buddhism. Buddha's story doesn't have any killing at least. How do you expect peace without a peaceful story? Give me a peaceful story any day."

# CHAPTER 7

Varti was starting to smoke. Teaching me to guide tours wasn't enough. Maybe, she said, she should remarry and have six children after all.

"You could do worse," Meri said hopefully. "There are lots of men who would want you, if you didn't dress as though you weren't interested."

"There's nothing wrong with the way I dress," Varti said. "Pants are traditional Armenian garb. I'm keeping up the Armenian tradition. Not to mention the Chinese, the Indian..."

"We wore beautiful pants. You're wearing Joe's pants."

A letter from Varti's father arrived. He was writing, he said, without telling her mother. Her mother wasn't well. The separation from Varti was eating her up.

"Right," Varti said. She threw the letter out.

I was throwing Ara's letters out, too. I hadn't answered him since he blamed me and Varti for the demise of the Armenian nation. I came back from taking lunch to Uncle Samuel one afternoon, and there he was, lounging under the pepper tree.

"What are you doing here?"

"Letters aren't enough," he said. "After a while, I wasn't sure you were real."

He had brought me a gift, a book which would deepen my knowledge of Armenian art, foster my Armenian pride, keep me in the fold. It was a book on Armenian carpets with photographs and drawings of medallions, stylised dragons' heads and crosses, empty plains and hidden valleys. Of special note, he said, was the history of the word "carpet," direct descendant of the Armenian *kapert* (I would find references to *kaperts* in Armenian texts as early as the fifth century). Florentine merchants imported *kaperts*, both flat-woven and knotted, from Armenian towns.

He had to tell me this, of course. The book was in Armenian.

"Give it to an Armenian girl," I said. "I can't read Armenian."

Aunt Gracia's voice floated into the garden: "He has no business interfering with your memories." She was speaking Turkish.

"What did she say?" Ara said.

"She said you're very thoughtful."

"I don't think so. She'll never let you marry me if she doesn't like me."

"Marry? Who does he think he is barging in like that? In my day, no boy would have been so presumptuous." She had switched to French, a courtesy she had never offered Aimée under any circumstances. He didn't seem grateful. He left.

That night I dreamed of a river, a ribbon of light twisting through russet mountains. Uncle Samuel said dreaming of water was good luck. I wanted water to be good luck.

Now Varti's mother wrote, and it was her father who was being eaten up by her silence.

"Gee," Varti said. "That's weird. Don't they talk to each other?"

Mariam wrote. She had a new plan. Ami Zaven didn't need a brother. What he needed was a wife. Meri was a widow, wasn't she? An Armenian widow. Then Ami Zaven wrote. Who was this Varti Gordon? How had she come to be in Jerusalem? How had her father come to be in Canada?

"You've got his hopes up," Varti said.

"What's wrong with hope?" I said.

"Nothing," she said. "I just don't have any. The world is a mess, and I'll never drive a cab again. The romance has run out of it."

"You're afraid, that's all."

"I know I'm afraid, pipsqueak. So what? The romance has still run out of it."

I dreamed of the river again. The water was still and dead, a dark unmoving line against the mountains. The russet slopes were arid. The next time Ara came, he wanted to know what it had been like growing up in the enemy country, learning their lies, speaking their language.

"You're as bad as the Turks who say all Armenians have narrow foreheads and sneaky souls. We're not that different from each other, you know. We wear the same clothes, we weave the same cloth, eat the same salads, and get married off by our parents. We all went to the same schools, and we even went to the same baths. Imagine that."

"You don't like to agree with me, do you?" he said. "There is no similarity between Armenians and Turks. The Turks have always been a cruel, ruthless people hated the world over. No one respects a Turk."

"Then why are we known the world over for our overwhelming hospitality? A Turk will not only bring up six other starving children, they'll put up a total stranger for months."

"What did I tell you?" Aunt Gracia said from behind the curtains. "He wants to change your memories for you. If you marry that boy, you won't be happy a single day of your life."

"You're worrying for nothing," I said.

"Everything I ever worried about was something to worry about, believe me."

I trapped Ara in my camera, a tiny figure smiling in a tiny circle of glass, and gave him to her. "There," I said. "Now you can do what you want with him."

One morning, Varti perched on my bed. I was just getting up. She had just come home. She had taken another mission that had involved her car; nothing dangerous, she said, nothing like picking up a stranger in broad daylight. "Have you had sex? No, of course you haven't. What am I thinking of? You probably haven't even kissed. He's so proper and respectful. Good thing, too. What if you got pregnant? Then where would you be? Up the creek without a paddle, that's where. Sorry, kid. Ignore me. It just goes to show where my mind is. In bed. Anybody's. I think I'm becoming a woman of loose morals. I never used to be a woman of loose morals. Or at least, I'd like to be a woman of loose morals."

"Women of loose morals can get pregnant."

"Women of really loose morals don't get pregnant. They use diaphragms. Or they have abortions. Nice women get pregnant."

"What's a diaphragm?" I said. "What's an abortion?"

"Right," she said.

And condoms. She could bet her bottom dollar that I didn't know what they were, either. Sure as shooting, Ara wasn't going to turn up with any. That was exactly how these things happened. Of course, if things started to go too far, I could simply whisper the word "pregnant" or "baby" into his ear, and that should cool him down pretty quick. But who was going to whisper in my ear? Girls wanted sex just as much as boys. Who was going to stop me? Sex was normal. It wasn't normal to not have sex. Believe me, she knew. And someday if I was lucky, I would know, too.

Aimée wrote. She wanted to send Mariam for a visit, but Mariam kept finding excuses not to leave. Then Mariam wrote. She hoped I wouldn't be angry, but Nissim was a kind, wonderful, generous, thoughtful person, and if I had changed my mind about him, she would understand.

I didn't understand.

"Wow! Wedding bells," Varti said. "She wants to marry him, and Mariam's mother wants to get her out of the country. Pronto. Stay tuned."

"Mariam always was sensible," Aunt Gracia said. "She'll never have to worry a day of her life with that man. Which is something that you would think about if you were smart instead of wasting your time on a boy who doesn't know if he's coming or going."

"He's not a boy. He's twenty years old. And he does know if he's coming or going. He's a photographer. He's working with his father in Jaffa. Anyway, Mariam can't marry Nissim. All her babies will be dead."

"Don't be silly," she said.

I dreamed about Mariam married. The Nissim in my dream wasn't the Nissim puffing up the hill. He was taller. Proud. Masterful. I wrote Mariam back to tell her that she had to bring Ami Zaven to meet his relatives: the only way he would come was if she told him she wanted to see her grandparents and needed someone to come with her. They weren't getting any younger.

And I said that I hadn't changed my mind.

Then I mailed Ami Zaven the book on Armenian carpets, my apology, I said, and a gift from a nice Armenian boy. It was bait.

There was another letter for Varti, this time signed by both her parents. They had just discovered that they had each written to her, that they were both being eaten up, and why hadn't she told them that she had almost been killed? How long did they have to pretend they didn't know Joe was dead? Did she think they were so heartless?

"Who told them I was almost killed?" Varti said. "Who's going behind my back?"

"Nobody," Meri said.

"Right," Varti said.

Ara wanted me to meet his parents. If we going to be married, I would have to meet them some day.

"Who said we're getting married?" I said. "You don't marry just because you love someone."

"You don't?"

"No."

"Why not?"

I didn't know why not. Varti hadn't told me that part.

I shrugged and tried to look knowledgeable.

# CHAPTER 8

A ra and I were in the kitchen. It was hot August. Upstairs, the open casement windows caught the mountain cool, but downstairs, there wasn't any to catch. Ara wanted to go out to the garden and look at the moon, the crescent moon, symbol of hope and promise. He wanted to go out and cool off.

"Hope?" I said. "Promise? How can you call something that looks like a hand scythe a symbol of hope and promise?"

"I see. The hand scythe that murdered your parents. You think the crescent moon belongs to Turkey. The moon doesn't belong to Turkey, do you understand? You're not going to give them that, too. They've taken enough."

He pulled me up and led me out to the garden.

"We're going to sit here until you see that there's nothing to be afraid of." The crescent moon was rising through the olive branches, threading its way upward through the slender silvered leaves. It would break free, rising ever higher, until, finally, raised by an invisible, powerful arm, it would strike.

I was looking at the moon, and Ara was looking at me. "You see?" he said. "It's not a knife. It's one of your curls, floating just out of reach..." He was playing with a curl, following the line of my neck with his breath. I curled in to his warmth, to his touch, to his lips, to his hand on my back, on my belly — I felt myself melting and urgent and open under his hand. And then he came into me, and it was — surprising, odd, that he should fit — that this was — sex. It was sex. What Varti was always talking about. Sex.

I wanted his hand back.

Twigs were digging into my back. An ant crawled over my leg. I loved his weight on me.

I remembered what else Varti had said. Diaphragm. Condom. Pregnant. Baby. Maybe the first time, you couldn't get pregnant. Maybe it took practice. That's why people "tried."

I sat up. He fell off with a peaceful smile under that silver scrap moon.

Married people "tried." Unmarried women were loose women.

But sex was natural. You couldn't be loose if it was natural.

"It's natural," I said. "Sex is natural."

"How do you know?" he said.

"Didn't it feel natural?"

"Nothing ever felt like that before."

A month later, I started eating tomatoes. Fresh tomatoes. Dried tomatoes. Canned tomatoes. Tomato sauce. Tomato soup. I dreamed of tomatoes. I dreamed of babies. Babies that looked like Ara, babies that looked like Uncle Samuel, babies that looked like Varti, and babies I had never seen before. Babies with blue eyes and babies with brown eyes, babies that gooed and babies that cried. My breasts hurt. My itty-bitty squingy breasts. They felt bigger. They felt strange.

I told Varti.

"Oh, my god," she said. "You're pregnant. I can't believe you knew enough to become pregnant. I mean, who told you? Armenians never talk about sex. It's my fault. I should have

told you more about birth control. Birth control is natural,
too, you know. I wasn't any smarter than your aunt. I was
playing ostrich. I'm responsible. Oh, my god. It's all my fault.
Does Ara know? What do you want to do? I know a woman
who's great with herbs. It's not a baby yet. It's only the
possibility of a baby."

"But if sex is natural, aren't babies natural?"

"Not when you're only fifteen and unmarried. Of course
by then you'll be sixteen. Which doesn't make it any better
in my books."

"I don't dream about dead babies, though," I said.

"Dead babies? You dream about dead babies?"

"Maybe I'm not pregnant," I said. "Maybe I just like
tomatoes."

"Yeah," she said. "Right."

Ara hadn't been back. He wrote letters. He was staying
away so that he could learn to control himself. He didn't want
Aunt Gracia and Uncle Samuel to think he didn't respect me.
He didn't want them to think he was rushing me. He wanted
them to like him.

He thought of me all the time.

I was still eating tomatoes, tomatoes growing fully,
deliciously, on the vine.

"What are you going to do, Sosi?" Varti said. "Sooner
or later, you're going to have to face it."

"I am facing it," I said. "I'm the one with sore breasts
and a crampy stomach. I'm the one everybody's going to hate.
I'm the one who's a loose woman."

"I told you," Varti said. "Only nice girls get pregnant.
You're a nice girl, and don't you forget it, and where the hell
is that boyfriend of yours at a time like this?"

We went to see him. Now that I was pregnant, Varti
wouldn't let me drive: you never knew with pregnant women
— they could throw up or become dizzy at any moment.

I hadn't thrown up or become dizzy. I only ate tomatoes. At least when I was driving, I didn't think about tomatoes.

"Will Ara hate me?" I said.

"He'd better not," Varti said. "I'll cut off his testicles."

The shop was on a narrow lane leading to the sea. I could hear the water slapping at the wall, I could smell the salt air. The light was vibrant, ginger and salt and lemon and heat. Ara wanted me to come in to meet his father. I didn't want to meet his father. I couldn't. How could I meet the grandfather of my illegitimate baby?

"Baby?" he said.

"You know," I said. "The moon."

"The moon?"

"Us under the moon."

"Us under the moon?" He looked surprised. Pleased. Guilty. "It's my fault."

I burst into tears. He stood watching me. He didn't hold me. He didn't kiss me. He wiped my eyes with his shirt.

No one would marry us. The one Armenian priest Ara knew in Israel wanted to know why we were in such a hurry, and Ara wouldn't lie because Armenians had been fighting against lies since 1915. The Catholics and Anglicans and Greek Orthodox and German Lutheran wouldn't marry us because we weren't Catholic or Anglican or Greek or German or Lutheran, and we couldn't lie about that, either.

Ara wrote every day. Was I feeling sick? Was I throwing up? Was I worrying too much? Was I eating? Was I sleeping? Did I miss him? Was I sorry? Did I love him as much as he loved me? Was I as happy as he was?

"Gee," Varti said. "Who would have thought being pregnant and unmarried at sixteen would be so romantic."

"Varti," I said. "No one will marry us. What are we going to do?"

"Oh," she said. "Right. Well — lie. If you give a good enough story, somebody should be willing to do it."

"We can't lie. Not according to Ara, anyway."

"I see. Not desperate enough yet. Okay. Well, I never thought being married was such a big deal anyway. How much more married could you be?"

When Ara finally came to see me again, I told him we couldn't make love until we were married. I was sorry as soon as he left. I spent the rest of the day imagining his hands all over me while I ate jars of canned tomatoes. Then I received a letter. If I had changed my mind about marrying him, he would understand. A man was supposed to protect a woman. He had betrayed me.

"Did he betray me?" I asked Varti.

"Damn right," she said.

"But I liked it."

"Yeah, and you're pregnant. He's not."

I became weepy, eating dried tomatoes with olive oil and parsley and basil and weeping.

"What's the matter with you?" Aunt Gracia demanded.

"She's pregnant," Varti said. "She's pregnant, and she's married to Ara, and you're going to be a grandmother. She's been afraid to tell you."

The floor opened up. A three-headed dragon and eunuchs with scimitars were dancing out of it. I waited for Aunt Gracia to grab one of the scimitars.

"When did she get married?"

"Last Christmas when we went into the old city."

"Right from under my nose," Aunt Gracia said. "They stole her right from under my nose."

"Nobody stole me," I said. I wiped a tear and nibbled at another slice of dried tomato.

"Why didn't you tell me? Didn't you think I would want to be at your wedding? Do you think I want you sneaking off and marrying like an orphan? What kind of person do you think I am?"

"I'm sorry," I said.

"I suppose everyone knows but me," she said glumly.

"No," I said. Varti was letting me lie for myself now. "Nobody knows we're married. Even Meri doesn't know."

"Oh," she said with relief. "You mean I'm the first one? Hasn't he told his parents either?"

"No," I said.

"When am I going to be a grandmother?"

"In six months."

"But you're so young!"

"You're not going to cry, are you?" I said. "Can't you just yell at me?"

"You're only a baby. I've spent so many years worrying about you..."

"You can still worry about me. I'm terrified."

"Why?"

"I'm having a baby."

"That's the easy part, believe me. The trouble starts after they're born."

"But it'll be dead," I said.

"Where did you get that idea?"

"Dead baby dreams," I said. "When you were trying to make me marry Nissim, I kept dreaming about dead babies."

"Don't be silly. You didn't like him. Nobody has dead babies. You're a healthy girl." She sounded depressed. "My own daughter, and I couldn't go to her wedding. What was it like?"

I made it up, combining the ceremonies I had seen in Father Havonissian's church with the opulence of St. Gregoire's chapel in the old city. The cross Ara's godfather held between us as the priest performed the ceremony was of chased silver; the chain laid over our heads linking us in the eyes of God was a rope of gold. The wine goblet we drank from, first Ara's godfather, then Ara, then my godmother, then me, was inlaid with garnets, rubies, sapphires, emeralds, and pearls. The church was filled with incense, and the chanting filled the skies.

"Who was your godmother?"

"Did I say godmother? Sorry. I didn't have one. I didn't know anyone to ask besides Varti, and she wouldn't. She said she had given me enough advice already."

"You'd better get one. There are some things parents never like to talk about with their children. I always thought the Armenian custom of waiting until marriage to choose your godparents is the smartest. At least that way you have some say over who's going to be meddling in your life." She kissed me on the top of my head. "Well, what's done is done. You have to tell your uncle. It's not fair to hide things from him."

I wanted Varti to tell him. She was so good at it. She wouldn't. She had gotten me out of trouble, and I could do the rest myself. Besides, it was only a technicality. All that was missing was the piece of paper.

"Uncle Samuel," I said. "I have shocking news."

"There is nothing you can say that will shock me."

"I'm married."

The earth opened up again.

"You didn't have to hide. Your aunt's bark is worse than her bite," he said.

"No," I said. "It wasn't that I was afraid. I'm going to have a baby."

And then I cried. He held me, and I cried.

I was beginning to look pregnant. I had a round belly and uncomfortable womanly breasts. Ara brought some of his mother's tomatoes preserved in olive oil. He had stolen them from her. I had used all ours up, every last bit. Aunt

Gracia looked at my belly, and then she looked at the jars sitting on the counter. "I suppose he'll be moving in soon, too," she said. "Him and his tomatoes." I hadn't thought about Ara moving in. I had mostly thought about where I could get more tomatoes. And my larger sore breasts. They were getting in the way. They were lumpy to sleep on.

I thought about him moving in. We would be together every day. He wouldn't like me. He would get tired of me with my bony body and I would never get tired of his lovely shoulders and his lovely bum. And Ami Zaven and Mariam were coming, Mariam who would never in a million years have become pregnant before she married. Ara would be sorry he wasn't marrying her instead. He and I would never be married now, anyway, because Aunt Gracia and Uncle Samuel thought we were.

The next time Ara came, Aunt Gracia announced that if we were already married, there was no point in sneaking around. We were in bed. Ara was stroking my bony shoulder and planning that our baby would be exactly like me. All I could think of was that it would be better for my baby if it were like Mariam instead, sweet, and gentle, and never causing a moment's trouble. "Oh, no," I said. "Not like me. You'll be sorry if it's like me."

"Young man, if that baby is even a bit like Sosi, you'll be the luckiest man in the world." It was Aunt Gracia from behind the bedroom door. "She has never given us a moment's unhappiness. She has a nature like a dove. Sweet like sugar. It's time she stopped that. She was full of imagination. I never knew what she was going to come up with next."

Varti and I were standing at the dock waiting for Mariam and Ami Zaven to disembark. It was cold, blustery, and grey. The sea was choppy, and Varti was angry: "As soon as that poor man takes one look at me, he'll know we couldn't be related in a million years. I should never have picked you guys up that day. You're going to be just like your aunt, a real little busybody."

Mariam and Ami Zaven were walking toward us.

"Holy mother of Mary," Varti said. "Good Lord, pipsqueak. What if you're right? Look at that — the same eyebrows, the same bald spot. They lean into the wind the same way. If you had shown me a picture, I wouldn't have known which was which."

"I did. You said everyone looked the same in pictures."

"On the other hand," she said, "we're from the same tribe. No wonder we all look alike."

Mariam, my perfect, gentle cousin, was softer and lovelier than ever. Her shining braids were gone. Her hair was short and bouncy and sophisticated. She was wearing a nubby tangerine silk sheath under a Canadian mink coat, an engagement gift from Nissim. I was in a shirt of Ara's over my favourite pedal pushers that were too tight and one of Aunt Gracia's coats. Suddenly, I wanted to tell her everything.

I took a deep breath. Mariam didn't understand secrets — if it was good news, you wanted everyone to be happy for you, and if it was bad, you needed all the help you could get. But they wouldn't help. They would make me give up the baby. That's what usually happened, Varti said; unmarried women gave their babies up for adoption. I didn't want to give my baby up for adoption. It would be an orphan. I didn't want my baby to be an orphan. I didn't want someone else to have my orphan baby. I lied.

"Guess what," I said. "I'm married, and I'm going to have a baby. You wouldn't have been able to come to the wedding, anyway. Jews aren't allowed into the old city. Besides, it kind of took me by surprise. I only knew him two days."

"Sosi! I'm surprised at you!"

I was surprised at me, too. I changed the subject.

"You're not really going to marry Nissim, are you? He doesn't deserve you."

"According to you, nobody deserves me."

"Nobody does. But somebody might more than Nissim. How can you stand to have him touch you?"

She blushed.

Maybe she was even pregnant. Maybe I had been wrong. Maybe she would in a million years get pregnant before she was married.

"You're not pregnant, are you?"

"How could I be?" she said.

"Oh, right," I said. "I forgot."


Aunt Gracia had been expecting an invitation from Ara's parents; we were, after all, guests in their country. Now, with Ami Zaven and Mariam here, she had an excuse to invite them.

" — Um," I said.

"He doesn't want us to meet them," she said. "They don't want to meet us."

" — Um — can't I meet them first?"

I told Ara I was coming to meet his mother. Mrs. Mamoulian didn't want to meet me. She didn't stand up, she didn't offer tea, and she didn't look at me.

"No respectable girl would have done what you did," she said. She was speaking to a gold icon on the wall. "Ara will regret his mistake."

"This is your son's child," I said. "Your grandchild."

She kept her eyes fixed on the icon.

"You can think what you want about me," I said. "But you can't think what you want about your grandchild. No one is ever going to hurt my baby. Especially not his grandmother."

She looked up. I left. I felt sick.

# Chapter 9

"Do you feel married?" I asked Ara. We were in bed. Nose to nose. I kissed him on his fingertips, behind his ear, inside his elbows. I crawled all over him, kissing him. He was stroking my belly.

"I wouldn't feel married even if we were," he said. "You still live with your family, and I still live with mine."

"Lots of people live like that. Aisha Hanim didn't see her husband for a year at a time."

"He was a sailor. I'm a photographer."

I stopped kissing him. If we were married, he would make me live with his mother. He could do that. He could do what he wanted with me. Daughters are born to bring light to another home. Marry a daughter, lose a daughter; marry a son, gain a daughter. His mother would work me from dawn to dusk, beat me, starve me, so that I would be too weak to feed my baby, and it would become skin and bones and die. Ara would be a widower. Everyone would feel sorry for him, and he would be married off in a week and live happily ever after, and I and my baby would be dead.

I slept on my side of the bed. It was lonely.

"Good lord," Varti said the next morning, "what's going on with you two? You look terrible."

"It's over," I said. "Our unmarried marriage is finished."

"That quick? What happened? Didn't you make love last night? It's no big deal, you know. All newlyweds are devastated the first time they miss a night. Wait till you haven't made love for nine months. Or a year. Or two. People get tired, you know. They get sunburns. The passion wears off. They have meetings too late. There are chickens to feed and onions to plant."

"Ara works in Jaffa," I said.

"So?"

"So he'll make me live with him. And his mother."

"His mother despises you."

"I know, but I'm his wife, remember?"

"No one is going to make you do anything you don't want to do, kid. I guarantee it. He can live here with your mother. Jaffa is barely an hour away — fishmongers get to the Jaffa docks and back here to the market every morning by eight. And when things are slow at his dad's, he can help us out. Meri could use him. He knows eight times more about photography than any of us do."

It was true. He did. Ara had his first camera when he was six; he was developing his own photographs when he was ten; he knew how to compose and crop, print and tint, and knew it much better than Meri still. But things were never so busy that three people were needed.

"There isn't that much work," I said. "You're up to something. You look sneaky."

"I don't look sneaky. I look responsible. Dad wants me to bring Zaven to Montreal."

"But you hate it there," I said. "You hate the weather, your friends are all married, and there are too many dull moments."

"Not anymore. I've reformed. Me and your aunt, we're on the same team. The more dull moments the better. Anyway, it's only going to be for a few months."

She was nervous, too. She wasn't sure she was ready to give up her independence now that her parents were ready to forgive her.

"What independence? At least there are only two of them. There are five of us."

"Maybe there is safety in numbers," she said.

I saw my baby in a dream. She was lying on Mama's headscarf, tiny, helpless, waving her arms to be picked up. Mama stood over her, looking down on her with eyes filled with longing. The infant turned to me, but I was frozen, locked behind my dream. Then she was with Uncle Samuel, able to stand now, on his lap, stretching for his glasses as he leaned back against the olive tree in our courtyard. Suddenly, he was slipping off the bench onto the pebbled ground, trying to protect her as he fell. She laughed. She thought it was a game. When she finally had the forbidden glasses in her hand and he didn't respond, she screamed in terror.

I woke up out of her terror.

I wanted Ara. I wanted my dark-eyed passionate husband. I wanted him in me, and on me, and around me.

I wanted him to tell me that it was just a dream.

I lay there wanting Ara, and my baby wasn't kicking. It hadn't kicked all day. I sat up. Nothing. I rubbed my belly. Nothing. I stood up. I bent over. I did a somersault. I stood on my head. Nothing. No pokes at the belly button. No jabs at the ribs. I had killed my baby. I had left it crying, and now it was dead.

Aunt Gracia stood in the doorway: "What are you doing? Stop that! You could lose the baby!"

"My baby's dead," I said.

She slapped my stomach. Hard. The baby banged back. "Don't scare me like that," she said.

I spent the rest of the night and all day making sure the baby was kicking and trying to feel if it had all its parts. Babies had so many parts. What if it was missing an ear or a leg? What if it was missing toes or a nose?

"For heaven's sake, let it get some sleep," Aunt Gracia said. "And that husband of yours, when is he moving in? The baby isn't deaf in there, you know. It will be born knowing our voices — and not his. He'll pick her up, and when he looks in her eyes he will see, 'Who are you? Give me back to Grandmamma.' He won't like that, I can tell you."

Ara moved in, and he brought maps. No one would ever do to our child the wrong that had been done my mother and me. Our child would be born knowing Armenian history. After we made love — sometimes before, while he nipped at my breasts or behind my ears, history lessons confused by the mists of desire — he talked at my belly about us, our beginning, the Hayk, descendants of Noah's first grandson clustered around Mount Ararat. (We were *Hayk* plural, and *Hay*, singular, to ourselves; *Armini* to the Persians; *Armenioi* to the Greeks.) He traced tiny sheep on the growing mountain of my belly.

Most of the prenatal lessons were inspired by the map of the Armenian Golden Age, lively kings and queens and carpets and castles peppering Greater Armenia sprawling from the Black Sea to the Mediterranean Coast. Tigran the Great battled his way across my back and around my breasts, conquering an ever-expanding territory that endured from the 1st century AD to the 5th century AD. Our child would be born with the blood of fighters. Our child tumbled in my tummy under the glow of a mighty past.

Later maps, as Armenia shrank and lost coastlines, were drawn in progressively darker colours, and by the Middle Ages, "Greater" had dwindled to "Little," Little Armenia, complete with stubborn stone churches, clung to the Mediterranean. Yet the more Armenia shrank, the more my baby and I had to learn. Those humble churches, the ruins of which were on the Anatolian plateau today, were testimony to Armenian creativity. Intellectual thievery. Clever marketing. For it was the inspired builders of our humble stone churches who first used the crossed knave, later translated into the colossal, arrogant, overdone cathedrals of Europe.

Finally, we disappeared altogether — almost 600 years, 1375-1918 AD — with no Armenia at all. There was a map, nonetheless. Pale lines shadowed our varying shapes and forms across the Levant with a legend of religious revolts, embattled Christians in a sea of Islam who managed to reassert themselves for eight brief years, 1722-30. And then gone. Like a falling star.

Our defeats were whispered in my ear, lessons too dangerous for a child who must be born with hope. I fought back by stroking, biting, declining Armenian verbs, quoting incorrect facts — diversionary tactics. I wanted stories about princes and princesses, after the battles had been fought, before intrigue and murder and betrayal and battle.

The last map was tacked on the wall above the trunk opposite the bed so we could always see it, so that we could never forget. Beige. The colour of faded dreams. Armenia,1918-20. Armenia betrayed. Turkish Armenia, home to Armenians for thousands of years, no matter what the border or colour of the maps, had been 147,630 square kilometres, almost five times the area of the 29,800 square kilometers of the present Soviet Armenia.

Mount Ararat, our ancient home, loomed across the border, taunting us from Turkey.

I drew my own map, a village beside a crystal river and beyond an oleander ravine. An old man lived there who railed at the ungodly ways of men — and a child who loved him with the violence of a summer sun.

Ara and I had another fight. We had taken our blankets outside to make love under the moon because I was the moon, beautiful, delicate, round with a round moon belly, but then he wanted to name the baby after me, so that she would be like me, chasing goats and causing trouble.

If we named it after me, it would have my life. Mama's life.

"Anyway," I said, "it's going to be a boy, and you can't name a boy 'Sosi.'"

"Sorry," he said. "The dream was a girl. We'll name her after Mariam. That way she'll have a sugar almond life, but she'll still climb trees and chase goats. We'll get a goat just so she can chase it."

"I don't want her to be like me at all. Promise me if it's a girl and I die that you won't name her after me."

"Die?" he said.

"Women die in childbirth, you know. Lots of them. Half the time the babies die, too."

"Die?" he said again.

He stayed awake making sure his two girls didn't die. I went back to sleep. And I didn't dream.

"It's so romantic," Mariam said eyeing my belly covetously, "having a husband to fight with and a baby to worry about. I can hardly wait."

"You don't have to marry Nissim just to have a baby, you know," I said.

"I don't know why you think he's going to make me miserable," she said. "He adores me."

"Everybody adores you," I said. "You don't have to marry Nissim to be adored. You didn't like him when I was supposed to marry him. How can you like him now?"

"I never said I didn't like him."

"Mind your own business, Sosi," Aunt Gracia said. "When have you ever known Mariam to be unhappy about anything? Except you, that is."

Mariam and I got back from the market one morning with a lonely cabbage, two onions, and a fat fish — about the only things both unrationed and, now, in the middle of winter, available. Aunt Gracia was sitting outside in the shadowed light of the garden. It was a clear sparkling desert mountain day. She had been crying. Uncle Samuel wasn't sleeping. He couldn't breathe lying down, and he couldn't sleep sitting up, and he wouldn't go to a doctor. In all their years together, he had never spent a day in bed, never missed a day at the shop.

Today for the first time, he hadn't come down. "I'm scared to look," she said. "Go up and see if he's all right."

We went to see. He was lying there with a newspaper collapsed across his chest. As soon as we had arrived in Jerusalem, while I was struggling with Armenian, he had begun relearning the national language — the Hebrew of the hallowed texts now used to describe fish prices and sneak attacks. But then, he said, the hallowed language had always been used to describe sneak attacks. The Bible was full of them. It was just that from this far away, centuries later, they seemed poetic. Like Ara's maps.

Ara's maps didn't seem poetic. They seemed dangerous. Like my dreams.

He was awake.

"I suppose Gracia sent you to make sure I was still alive," he said.

Ami Zaven refused to go to Montreal now. "Why? What are you waiting for?" Uncle Samuel said. "Are you waiting for me to die? You'll never meet your brother, your carpets will rot in Turkey — just because you're waiting for me to die. In the meantime, Sosi's baby will grow up and be married, and you and I will be waiting for each other to die. What kind of life is that?"

"I have a right to be with you," Ami Zaven said. "After all these years, I have a right."

"Zaven," Uncle Samuel said — he held Ami's hand: "You have a right to live, too."

"But you know, Sam," Ami said. "After all these years, he may not want a brother. Who knows what we really remember? And what about the brother I have had all these years? Are we forgetting this brother? Aren't I Sosi's ami? 'Ami' — this is the father's brother, not the mother's brother. Who can say that it was an accident that this word came to my lips?"

He couldn't go. Turkey was the only home he knew. He was too old for a new life. Maybe the dream had been enough. Aunt Gracia and Uncle Samuel might want to stay in Israel, since I had married an Armenian Israeli, but, even so, with the surrounding Arab nations still determined that Israel had no right to exist, and the Israeli military bulldozing Palestinian homes, what kind of future was there? It wasn't such a bad idea to stay in Turkey so we would have a home to go back to.

We had failed on all counts. Through all those long discussions at Uncle Samuel's bedside between Ami and Meri and Uncle Samuel, the idea of a romantic alliance between Meri and Ami Zaven hadn't occurred to anyone, and Mariam and I were under orders from Varti to keep our lips buttoned. With Ami determined to go back to Turkey with Mariam, Varti would have to face the parents who hadn't spoken to her since her marriage to Joe, that nice non-Armenian boy, on her own. She couldn't pull out of the trip now.

A telegram arrived for Mariam: "Love you. Miss you. Marry me. Now." She beamed. Quietly. Nervously. When she walked up the ramp of the plane behind Ami to go back and tell Nissim she would marry him, she looked excited. The wedding would be as soon as possible — as soon as Uncle Samuel felt well enough to travel. A second telegram arrived: Nissim was offering plane tickets for all of us, his wedding gift to Mariam.

"If they wanted us to be at their wedding," Ara said, "they would get married here. Meri's right. Inviting us back to Asia Minor is like walking into the lions' den."

"What's wrong with you?" I said. "People, even Armenian people, go in and out of Turkey all the time. Just because we don't get permission to repair a church doesn't mean we get thrown into jail as soon as we cross the border. Besides, I still have a Turkish passport. I'm still a Reijskind, and I'm going with Reijskinds."

I wanted to go. I wanted to go home. And I wanted Ara with me. I would be going alone. Pregnant.

Uncle Samuel wasn't getting better. He needed more time, he said. After my baby was born, they would go back for a visit, maybe for good. Aunt Gracia wouldn't go without him. She was afraid of what she would find when she returned. Mariam was willing to put off the wedding. Nissim wasn't. He was over thirty. He didn't want to wait any longer. Uncle Samuel agreed. But there was no reason that the rest of us couldn't go.

Then Aisha Hanim wrote. Or, rather, Mariam wrote for her: Aisha Hanim had beaten her breast and torn her hair over me, bled for me, lost child of the mountains. To abandon her now in her old age was to spit on her swollen breast and our shared Turkish blood.

"Ha!" Aunt Gracia said. "Shared Turkish blood. In the meantime, she never once had to give up a night's sleep for you, she never fought with teachers and mothers. Any fool can beat her breast and tear her hair. All the years I gave to that woman, and now she slaps me in the face with her 'shared blood.'"

"What am I going to do, Uncle Samuel?" I said. "I feel like I've been cursed with both of Solomon's mothers, only neither of them would fail the test."

Uncle Samuel exploded, scattering newspapers all over the room. "Go!" he said. "I get sick once in my life, and all of a sudden no one can go anywhere."

Meri picked up the papers. She had come in for tea and to report on the latest unreasonable customer. Sometimes there was more creativity required than she was capable of. She needed the magic that gave Uncle Samuel's silk endless stretch, for photographs, it seemed, were expected to portray the beauty and youth of the inner soul, not the reality of the wrinkles or the pain or the emptiness wrought by life. Who would have thought that taking pictures could be so depressing? How had Krikor stood it? Personally, she would have chosen landscapes. Without people. Unspoiled. Peaceful.

"Go," Meri said. "Aisha Hanim deserves it. Gracia will survive."

Ara arrived then with falafels and proofs of me pregnant, Meri peering at negatives, Uncle Samuel buried in newspapers. The only one he couldn't get was Aunt Gracia. Meri presented the verdict: I was going to the wedding, and why wasn't he? He said he would talk to his wife privately.

He had to wait until we were in bed and sure that Aunt Gracia was asleep: "You're going without me? I'm your husband. You can't."

"We're not married yet."

"We've always been married," he said. "Before time. We were meant. We were only waiting."

"In that case, everything was meant. Our whole history. Not a pretty thought for one who believes in a just and merciful god."

"You don't want to marry me," he said.

"I never said I didn't want to marry you. No one will marry us. Anyway, according to you, we're already married."

"That's not the point. The point is that you don't want to marry me." He was breathing in my ear, sneaking down inside my nightgown, nipping tender breasts.

"I do want to marry you. I don't want to marry your mother. It means I belong to her for as long as she lives, and she'll live a long time. She's mean. What I'm asking is a lot easier than what you're asking me. If you loved me, you would come with me. Mariam told Father Havonissian about you. Don't you think he deserves to see you with his own eyes after battling with Aunt Gracia over my soul all those years?"

He stopped nipping. Suddenly he loved me a lot. Endlessly. Boundlessly. So much that he would follow me to the ends of the earth: "Of course," he said. "Father Havonissian will win. He'll marry us — even if it's just to spite her."

"She won't be spited. She thinks we're already married, remember? Besides, you just said we were married enough."

"We can never be married enough," he said.


We rose up and over the desert coast, up and through clouds. As we approached the yellow ochre shores of Mediterranean Turkey, the sea shimmered patterns of emerald and aqua. The river spilled darkly out of the land.

"Imagine," Ara shouted over top of the engines. "You came out of the mountains on a donkey, and ten years later you're going back in an airplane."

I didn't need to imagine. And I couldn't imagine anything more illusory. Nothing mattered that high up. From that high up, the world was a pattern in a carpet. From that high up, one could imagine making one's own patterns.

From that high up, one could believe in escape.

Even birds never really escaped. Even birds had to come down some time.

# CHAPTER 10

We were coming down, watching toy size become life size, flying over fields and fig trees, camels and courtyards.

"So this is where they make decisions about whether we live or die," he said.

"You can't blame every Turk for what happened almost forty years ago."

"Your parents were murdered only ten years ago."

"You're upsetting the baby," I said.

He looked guilty.

When we went through customs in Adana, they welcomed us, Mr. and Mrs. Gordon, to Turkey and wished for my Turkish cousins a long and fruitful married life.

I took my passport back from Ara. I was Mrs. Joseph Gordon, Varti. Ara and I were married, but not as ourselves. I wanted to yell at him in Turkish, the language I knew best; instead, I had to mutter in French and hope that I looked like I was talking about lost suitcases. "You could have warned me. I could have said anything — your name, that Happy one, for instance. If I've got Varti's passport, what does she have? Am I in Canada and I don't even know it?"

"It's fake. Joe's is real. She didn't need it."

"Varti knows about this, and I don't? Is this the shared Armenian blood you keep talking about?"

"Varti trusts me. Unlike my wife."

I recognized the Nissim from my dream, tall. Proud. He raised my hand to his forehead reverently, welcoming me, the one closest to Mariam's heart, as though he had no recollection of me at all. Aisha Hanim took a look at my belly, and threw her hands up to Allah: I would have twenty children and be worn out and die by the time I was forty; I had wasted my education; I had disappointed my parents; I had disappointed her. She hadn't raised me for this.

"You always said education was a waste of time."

"Only for people with heads of wood. If I had gone to school, I wouldn't have to break my heart over other people's children or wait like a servant for my son."

Her son was coming back to teach grade three at my old school. He had failed to bring literacy to the plateau. The *imam* didn't want it. Arabic lessons to read the Koran were enough. Shearing sheep or market week or backgammon was more important. What would educated boys do with their education anyway? They would become dissatisfied with the life their fathers had lived for centuries. They would question their elders, and desert their parents as their teacher had deserted his. Like I had deserted her.

"I didn't desert you. I'm back."

"Back for what?" she said. "So you can leave me again?" She ignored Ara completely.

"Nice guy, that Nissim," Ara said. "I don't know why you didn't want to marry him." He hoped I wouldn't be sorry, he said. Nissim had a grounding quality which was lost on Mariam, who was as grounded as you could get and still be alive.

Ara told Father Havonissian the truth — all of it. Father Havonissian apologized for all the priests who refused to marry us. After all, the job of a man of religion was to help one with the business of living. He chuckled: nature had taken matters into its own hands. It was he, the arch-enemy, whom Aunt Gracia would have to thank for protecting her grandchild. Someday, he knew, she would. In the meantime, it was a secret which would delight him every day.

Ara thought I had good taste in priests and men I didn't marry. He and Father Havonissian and Nissim were together every day, drinking arak and discussing the political truth of the Cold War and the treachery of the Stalinist regime and whether Israel and the Arabs would ever be at peace and Armenians would be full citizens. Or whether we would be continually caught in the crossfire.

Mariam was planning my wedding, the food (lamb soup, *pilaf, baba ganoush*), the dress (blue silk to match my eyes and, to hide my belly, empire line, reminiscent of medieval Armenian queens). It was my second wedding, she and Father Havonissian both announced innocently: I had come back to be blessed by my community.

Aisha Hanim knew better, and she knew that there was still a chance for me not to betray my/our Turkish blood. When I suggested that babies needed fathers, she said she had brought hers up on her own and done fine. Men knew nothing, only took their pleasure. She hoped that Ara was good for that at least, giving pleasure and not only babies. If he were Muslim he would know: it was written in the Koran that men were one part desire, and women nine parts. A child who had suffered such a depth of grief and caused such grief could only be expected to become a woman requiring an equal depth of pleasure. Allah had not created all of us equal. And she hoped I wasn't one of those modern women who would forsake a midwife for a doctor. Men should not look on women in such a way. This was for a husband's eyes only. What could a man know, anyway, about bringing a child into the world, these creatures who could neither give life nor suckle?

Mariam's mother was doubly distraught. Both her babies married, and the one she would least have expected pregnant. What could have gotten into us?

"Sex," I said.

I wanted to go to a volleyball game. Mariam wasn't interested in volleyball games. She wanted to know if I had been nervous on my wedding night and why not. Then she wanted to know what it was like and why I liked it the first time — her mother said the first time women were mostly just surprised. Shocked, even. Disappointed. Left out. Wedding nights went down in the annals of the worst night of their lives.

"Varti says it's luck. Ara seems to like women's bodies and making love to them. She says most men are big lovable cowards who will cross deserts and do hand-to-hand combat with rabid camels before they'll ask a woman what to do, and we're just as bad because even if we are smart enough to figure it out for ourselves we don't have the courage to tell them."

I told her what Varti said women had to tell their husbands — unless they were one of the rare ones who had orgasms just by thinking about them.

"I could never tell Nissim that," Mariam said.

"You don't have to. Varti already did. She left a letter for me to send him the second you were officially engaged. It's your wedding gift."

I thought Mariam was going to cry. Now he would think of her 'like that,' and today of all days when they were going over to Aunt Gracia and Uncle Samuel's house to decide if they wanted to live there. She would have to stand in her grandparents' bedroom with Nissim and discuss beds. She wanted me to go with her.

"This isn't a team sport," I said. "It's a two-hander, and this is your big chance. If you seduce him, you won't have to be nervous on your wedding night."

She glared at me. It was an incipient Aunt Gracia glare.

When she came back, she looked mildly stunned, like a basket of oleander blossoms had fallen on her head.

"Varti must write good letters," I said.

"Mind your own business," she said.

Somehow, after Aisha Hanim's horror over my belly, and talking about orgasms and Mariam's bedroom, there didn't seem to be a good reason to go to a volleyball game. I couldn't even pretend to be able to jump. At least I hadn't dreamed about dead babies or about leaving my husband. Maybe Ara was right. Maybe we were already married. Mariam said we fought like it. She and Nissim were in perfect accord on all matters at all times.

Between Mariam and Father Havonissian, everyone who had ever known me had been invited: the volleyball team; voices from the baths; teachers I tortured and teachers I behaved for; my entire childhood — the barber who had cut my hair, the coffee shop owner who had given me riches, the cobbler, the repairer of carpets. Emek, stocky, freckled, and green-eyed. We shared odd eyes. We should have been friends.

The Armenian congregation was there. I didn't recognize most of them. I had gone to church with Ami, holding his hand, never looking up past boots or shoes. I didn't want to know them, these other Armenians who lived while my mother did not. None of them were like my aunts and uncles with the mountain vastnesses in their souls. They were a frightened, Mediterranean people. The remnants of terror. I hated them for their fear. I hated them for my fear.

Father Havonissian bound us before the Lord with a silver chain and the incense rose to the ceiling and curled, frozen, above our heads.

Aisha Hanim said it was a beautiful wedding, and blessed be Allah who had willed it that she should live to be present at the most important day of my life. Ara had given her his camera. She had a good eye, he said, for composition.

"Do you feel married?" Ara asked.

I did. I slept snuggled up to Ara, and it was home.

Mariam and Nissim's wedding was all white satin and lace with an unblushing unpregnant bride. They went to Beirut for their honeymoon. Mariam promised to send postcards. Mrs. Behar, triumphant, allowed me to raise her hand to my forehead. I wanted to tell her that it was meant to be.

Ara was having frightening dreams. A baby thrown into the air for target practice. A woman lying mutilated in a courtyard. The woman, he says, is me, the baby is ours. And he, nowhere, behind the dream, desperate. Then a grassland trail. A well. He looks into the well, and sees reflections of faces. Eyes. His mother's eyes. My eyes. He is walking on the trail, retracing his mother's steps. Someone is waiting. He is dreaming because someone is waiting.

We had to leave before his dreams became mine. I went over to Aunt Gracia's house and sat on the roof and looked up at the gulls wheeling patterns of white against the blue, an endless search against azure light.

By the time we got back to Jerusalem, Uncle Samuel was too weak to get out of bed. Meri had gone into the old city to see Arpi for Christmas. We had missed it. Ara wasn't sorry, he said; no one would risk two checkpoints and the possibility of having their baby born in Jordan when they had to come back to the grandparents living in Israel.

Aunt Gracia sat up with Uncle Samuel all night, willing him to sleep. During the day, I lay beside him, holding his hand while he spoke in whispers about how we are all guardians of life, and he and Aunt Gracia had been privileged to be mine. Ara ran back and forth from the shop feeding us all tea and lentil soup. Monsieur Abhessera, fellow magician, came to report on the business of magicians. Lengths of silk had been sold, shoes came in for repair, a man closed his shop in the evening and sat down to a peaceful dinner — what could be more magical than that?

Nothing, Uncle Samuel said. Nothing could be more magical than that.

I went into labour.

Ara stood beside me and turned pale. Aunt Gracia ordered him out: "She's not dying. She's having a baby."

"How am I going to do this, Aunt Gracia?" I said. "My stomach is so big. How is it going to get out?"

"You'll be surprised," she said.

I was. It was astonishingly, breathtakingly overwhelming, because there she was, a squiggly little thing, all sticky and mine, lying on my belly. Ara looked ten years older.

It was squeaking. "What's wrong with it?" he said.

"Nothing," Aunt Gracia said. We cleaned her and wrapped her and took her in to Uncle Samuel. She nestled against his side.

"So," he whispered. He smiled. "She looks just like me."

He died that night.

I called her Sammi.

# CHAPTER 11

"Well," Aunt Gracia said. "I don't have anything to live for." We were sitting outside in the garden in a warm afternoon sun. She was holding the baby. It squeaked.

"She should have a hat," Aunt Gracia said. "Babies should never be without a hat."

"She's hungry," Meri said. "Where's Sosi?"

I was right there. Back with the hat.

"How can you call her Sammi?" Aunt Gracia said. "Every time I look at her, I'll think of him." She had never expected Uncle Samuel to die first. He hadn't been sick a day in his life. He never even had colds. What business did he have going first? Why hadn't she let him die in peace? Up until the very last day, she had been fighting with him to eat, to try to walk, to keep his strength up. I had given her such a pretty Armenian name. Archaluz. Sun. Why was I calling her Sammi?

I didn't want to talk about why. While I had been calling her Sammi, Meri and Aunt Gracia had been fighting over a name. At six weeks old, Sammi was still unnamed. Aunt Gracia wanted 'Gracia': she was the grandmother, after all. It was a simple sign of respect. Meri was outraged: I was half

Armenian, and Ara was 100% Armenian, which made Sammi
75% Armenian. Gracia, 100% Spanish, was an affront, no
matter who it memorialized. Even Varti, thousands of miles
away, had an opinion. The least we could do was hang on to
our own names so that there was some echo of us in the world.
Her suggestion, Rhipsime, caused another battle, but this
time inter-Armenian. Aunt Gracia took sides only when she
could cause trouble. Rhipsime, Varti said, had been totally
ignored by our literate and learned, who were, of course, men,
the priests who recorded history as they saw fit. King Tridates
III was given sole credit for the conversion of the Armenian
nation, a conversion undertaken out of gratitude to St.
Gregory the Illuminator for curing him of his madness. As a
more tangible reward, King Tridates III also let St. Gregory
out of jail.

But St. Gregory was in jail in the first place because
King Tridates III had put him there for the crime of being a
Christian, and King Tridates III had gone mad (thought he
was a wild boar) because he had had the woman he professed
to love more than life itself (her life, as it turned out) stoned
to death. Rhipsime's crime was her stubborn refusal to marry
him, yet Rhipsime, ungrateful little Christian that she was,
had rejected King Tridates' offer of marriage only because he
was a heathen. From Varti's point of view, if King Tridates
had converted right at the start, Rhipsime would have married
him, she wouldn't have been stoned, he wouldn't have lost his
mind, and King T, newly softened by his own Christianity,
would have let Gregory out of jail. The only loser would have
been Gregory because he wouldn't have become St. Gregory
the Illuminator. Rhipsime might have. And she should be a
saint because of her role in all of this anyway, innocent cause
of King T's madness and conversion, and murdered in the
bargain. A martyr for the cause.

Ara did not take kindly to Varti's reading of history.

I didn't want my daughter named for a woman who had
been stoned to death. I named her for the god of the skies,

giver of life. Archaluz. Sun. I had so many names, more than I wanted, yet my mother had no name. When my grandfather rescued her, he had called her Armaghan, "gift" in Turkish, and then Arma because Armaghan was such a long name for such a small child, and that became her name.

Ara picked Sammi up and planted twelve kisses on her. He should have been in Jaffa, but he had woken up and looked down at that bundle of vulnerability sleeping between us, this tiny, mystical creature, this squiggling, wriggling child of coincidences, of improbabilities.

The improbability was my grandfather, the miracle of his anger. When he died, the lines of Mama's life, the boundaries between certainty and uncertainty, tore. She would call for me sometimes in sudden panic, and I would run to her, dreading her relief when I came into view, as though she hadn't believed that I was anything more than a child of her imagination.

Yet I didn't believe in Sammi. She had nothing to do with me, who I was or where I had come from. Aunt Gracia and Ara, though, recognized her instantly — walking with her, singing to her about her blanket and her bath, her button nose and her ten little toes. Ara spent less and less time in Jaffa. He had been waiting for her all his life, and he didn't want to miss any of the baby pleasures, the day she would roll over onto her belly, the day she would put her foot in her mouth

I had never waited for anything. After Papa, there had been nothing to wait for.

Sammi didn't burble and chirp to me like she did to them. She watched me. Even when she was on my breast, she watched, unblinking, solemn.

"She doesn't like me," I said.

"Don't be silly. At her age, she's desperate to like you. She needs you too much."

"Did you like them right away?"

"Who?"

"Your babies." Aunt Gracia had had two more after Maurice. Both had died, the first just after birth, the second, Esther, when she was five years old. She had wandered off and drowned in the river. When I had come, so many years after they had lost Esther, I had given them the chance to do it over. Love another child. Keep her from drowning.

"Sosi," she said, "you are going to love this child so much that it will frighten you. Your heart will crack in a thousand pieces a thousand times."

"How long does it take?" I asked. "Loving them?"

"It takes as long as a smile," Aunt Gracia said. "Give her to me. Don't even hold her when you think like that."

Ara was adding new songs to his repertoire, warrior songs about Archaluz marching through Armenian valleys and plateaus with her rubber duck (Varti had sent a rubber duck) and her stuffed camel (Aunt Gracia had turned a brown sock into a camel). Archaluz would live to be ninety-seven, the head of a great clan of Mamoulians, Mamoulians spreading to every corner of the earth to finally converge on Mount Ararat. Home again.

I would wake in the middle of the night to find him sitting up watching her. He understood now, he said, dying for another. He belonged to her. From now on, everything he did would be prefaced by, "Is it good for Sammi?"

While Sammi was learning to stand, triumphant, Mariam was sending photographic pregnancy reports. She beamed above her belly. So did Aisha Hanim's fifteen-year-old daughter-in-law, a devout child with the energy of a kitten and the heart of a dove whom Aisha Hanim protected from her son with the ferocity of a falcon. Tançin had been the only girl in the village allowed to go to school. She had learned nothing at all. She had fallen in love with her teacher instead, and he with her, and she continued to resist his efforts to educate her. One person reading in the family was enough.

Tançin was a surprise. Aisha Hanim had had no idea that Rafiq was married. At last, she had a daughter who would never leave her. Mariam didn't sound as though she missed me, either. She was too busy being delighted by each new stage of pregnancy, none of which, it seemed, involved tomatoes.

Varti had met a "guy," a very, very Christian guy who went to church, sang in church, didn't swear, and venerated her because she had lived in the Holy City. For the first time in her life, she looked at a man and thought of children. She thought of settling down. She had never "settled down" with Joe. Maybe you couldn't "settle down" in a country where you were always expecting your chair or your bed or your vegetable garden to be blown out from under you. Or in a country where you didn't belong. At least in Montreal everyone mostly didn't belong together. And speaking of not belonging together, there had been an influx lately of Armenians from the west coast of Turkey. Ami Zaven might have felt right at home. Not to mention the fact that he would have been warm — she'd forgotten how warm and cozy it could be inside a house in a snowy winter, unlike the Middle East where there was no indoor heat, just bone-chilling cold and damp.

"She lied," I said. "She isn't coming back. She ran away."

"Life goes on, Sosi," Aunt Gracia said. "Even without you."

It was the first time she had used my name as though it wasn't practice.

I was worried about her. She hadn't wanted to come to Jerusalem in the first place: she had come only because of Uncle Samuel. I was afraid to bring it up.

Since Sammi's birth, Ara had given up Armenian history for folk tales and wild promises. The button eyes on her camel would be replaced by amber, the red wool bridle by gold and silver threads. Life was easing up. There was less rationing. The country was ready for luxuries. Perhaps he should go to discuss a partnership with Nissim. There was no better location than Jerusalem. Being in the centre of three of the world's great religions was an advantage. We weren't taking advantage of our advantage. If we could somehow set up another shop in the old city too, we could be selling from Christmas to Ramadan to Easter and Passover to the High Holidays and back to Christmas. We would be dressing people for all three Sabbaths, the Muslims on Friday, Jews on Saturday, and sixty-seven denominations of Christians on Sunday. And that wasn't counting christenings, confirmations, name days, and weddings.

"See?" I said to Aunt Gracia. "You were wrong. He does know what he is doing."

"Sosi," she said. "When did I ever say Ara didn't know what he was doing?"

"Are you all right?"

"Of course," she said. "Why do you ask?"

I lay down to have a nap with Sammi. I was forgetting that there had been a time without her, beginning to believe that all of civilization and life had led toward my daughter. Before her, there was nothing. I couldn't believe I had produced life, cuddling, cooing, hugging, snuggling life. I was Artemis incarnate.

One night, I dreamt of Sammi alone in the garden, crying, and I couldn't get to her. When I woke up, my cat's eye popped out of its setting and rolled to a stop against Ara's shoe. I picked it up. It lay there, helpless, naked in my hand.

I woke Ara.

"There's something you're not telling me," I said.

"I wouldn't hide anything from you. You're the mother of my child."

"I know I'm the mother of your child. But there's something you're not telling me."

He breathed into my ear. I picked Sammi up before it was too late. "You'll wake the baby," I said. "No information, no sex."

He considered. Sex won, but only if I promised not to start building epic myths out of random facts. He had a new passport. He had been reborn as Robert Nazar Porter, Robert Porter for an American father, and Nazar for a Palestinian Muslim mother. It was something photographers could do. Take passport photos. Forge passports. His forged passport would get him into Turkey without suspicion. He was a simple buyer of silk taking advantage of the opportunity to snap a few photographs of a country laden with ancient Greek and Ottoman history. Of course, I was welcome to come along as the obedient wife holding her husband's cameras. No one would question someone whose wife bowed to Mecca five times a day — and spoke perfect Turkish.

"You're joking, I hope. The whole thing sounds suspicious. You're forgetting that everyone in Turkey isn't a Muslim fanatic. There are laws against it, in fact. If I bow down in the middle of the street to Mecca five times a day, that's what they'll think. That we're religious fanatics. Maybe even Saudi. We're not Arabs, you know. We don't even like Arabs very much."

"It doesn't matter. At least they'll never suspect you're Armenian. An Armenian doesn't know how to bow that low. We die first."

"So do Turks," I said. "We only bow to Allah. Dying without a fight isn't what we have a reputation for. We didn't grow from an insignificant tribe in the east to the Ottoman Empire in four hundred years by being afraid to die. Or by being afraid to kill, either."

Sammi woke up. Ara walked her to sleep telling her all about the might of ancient Armenia and how to tint photographs. He would bring her a treasure trove of our past and our present.

"Good luck," I said. "How do you plan to do that? Photograph churches that don't exist? Hunt down survivors hiding behind Turkish names? You won't be picked up by someone like my grandfather who just wants to go back to the mountains and raise sheep. The military is everywhere, and we're all afraid of them. Those new roads aren't being built to bring out wool — camels have been doing that for centuries. They're for the military. You're going to go in there, one lonely Armenian with a camera... What am I supposed to tell your father?"

"You don't have to tell him anything. He's the forger."

The walls of the bedroom fell away, and I was on a blue-flowered plain with blood stars.

I drove to Jaffa to talk to the forger. Ara took Sammi to Meri's shop with him. She was good for business, drawing in clients as she played in the window surrounded by photographs of herself — and diverting them from arguments over "so many shekels for just a piece of paper."

I had come to know the road to Jaffa, the twists and the turns, when the mountains become hills, where there were sand dunes. There was always a surprise. A ploughed field. A Bedouin camp. A hawk. Pure sunlight cactus flowers. The first glimpse of the sea.

Ara's father was sitting on the dock with a cigarette. He believed in making passports. It didn't matter who they were for or where they hoped to go. He made them for anyone, and he made them for free. Who was he to judge another man's fears or another man's dreams? Each of us had to be prepared for flight. If this century had taught us anything, then it should have taught us that. He didn't blame me for not understanding. I couldn't be expected to know, a child of peacetime. Ara, hardly older, knew because he had the honour of being God's chosen — chosen to live in the Holy Land, land of hope. Land of death.

I laughed. I tried to imagine a time before fear. Mama had been terrified all the time, and Papa was fearful for her.

Even my grandfather had said that a wise man knew when to walk in the shadows.

"You could stop him," I said. "He'll listen to you. Tell him you don't want to lose your last living son. Tell him he has no right to be playing games when he has a daughter."

"There are no games," he said. "Since he was a child, there have been no games. This is not a game. He tries to see a future for Sammi — Sammi in school, Sammi a mother, a grandmother. The film is blank. He thinks that if he brings back proof of the genocide, no one can ever deny it. It can't happen again."

"You don't expect me to believe that, do you? Only one country denies the genocide."

He shrugged. "I can't tell you what to believe, and I can't tell him what to do."

I started dreaming of empty moonlit plateaus, of blue flower eyes and blood stars, and always, in the background, there was the creak of the wooden water wheel, turning, creaking, turning. But there was no water. The riverbed was dry. Sunflowers turned their backs to the sun.

I told Ara my dream. I told him I didn't care what had happened to my mother. I cared what would happen to my daughter. He kissed me on the nose. He stroked my back. He called me his little moon-mad Armenian. He changed the subject. It was too easy for him to change the subject. When he touched me, my body forgot what my mind was talking about.

I remembered what Varti had said: "Marriage isn't all that it's cracked up to be."

I tried one last assault, while I still had any mind left at all: "Christianity started with a sect. Zealots in the desert. There might be one and a half million more Armenians in the world today if we weren't Christian. What's the difference between a good Armenian and a good Muslim, anyway? There is good and bad in every group, and I ought to know. I've got the blood of both. And so has your daughter."

He looked like I'd shot him.

I woke up one night, and Sammi was sitting up beside me calling for *Baba*. Ara was gone. There was a full moon. I wrapped her up and carried her out to the garden to show her the moon. "Look," I said. "We're all in a room lit by the moon." She turned to me, glowing, a tiny round face bathed in moonlight. She stretched a hand to touch the moonlight.

And my heart cracked.

# CHAPTER 12

Ara did send silk, charmeuse and crèpe, satin and georgette, raw silk, silk and linen, silk and cotton, silk and wool, silk like water, silk like love. Dusk grey. Moon-glow ivory, after-glow peach. Desert red and prickly pear yellow. Black. Shimmering, sensuous black. Enough for all the widows of all of Asia Minor.

Inside, wrapped in newspaper articles (Ataturk's birthday, projected record harvest, volleyball tournament, American ambassador visiting bazaar) were exposed rolls of film. Meri thought that I would want to help develop them. She thought I would want to share in Ara's voyage. Meri needed vistas, distance, and space. She hated dark rooms and studio work, yet Krikor could have shot the same person forever, exploring new angles and new lenses, dissecting seconds for nuance and mood.

"It's his film," I said. "Ara can develop it himself."

"Heavens," she said. "Anger overcomes curiosity. I was never able to do that. He's just trying to retrace your world, Sosi. You can't blame him for that. If nothing else, this will be a record for Sammi. You have to admit that it's magic — he's there, we're here, and we can see what he's doing."

The photographs looked innocent enough: Ara scooping up a handful of perfect oval eggs. (Silk cocoons.) A worn stone cat-like creature overlooking a vast plain. (A Hittite lion.) Carved columns against an empty sky. (Ionic.) Ara sitting on a pile of rubble. Ara in the midst of a flock of goats. I was starting to look forward to the photographs. Madame Abhessera was looking forward to the silk. She was beginning to do a good business with Ami's stock, and she had been running out.

Then the shipments ceased. The moon shattered.

"It's too soon to worry," Aunt Gracia said. "It's a miracle he's been able to send as much as he has. It's not as if there's mail out from every village every week."

Three months later, there had been no further miracles.

Aisha Hanim and I used to take food to those whom the prisons had spat out, men with misshapen limbs and mysterious scars, who clung to walls and slept in alleyways. Some were mad, some were incontinent. They all wondered why their bodies had betrayed them. Why they lived. *"Inshallah,"* Aisha Hanim would say. "As Allah wills."

I hated it when she said that.

Whenever an Armenian was put into prison, Father Hovanissian became frantic, desperately canvassing the shop owners on the square for money to buy them out. Prisoners killed each other as often as guards tortured them, and when one had nothing, everything was cause, an inadvertent glance or a usurped spot on the floor. An Armenian in prison had less of a chance than most; he was different, uncircumcised. Even Jews were circumcised. A Jew could pass for a Muslim. In prison, with a hundred men in a room, with a latrine in the corner, Ara wouldn't be able to hide if he tried, and he wouldn't try. I knew he would make enemies even of those who might not have been. Ara had a hundred speeches designed to incite: Armenians, the true native sons, had trusted traitorous Turks too often; Armenians had helped the Young Turks in the 1908 rebellion and been betrayed; there had been no room for us — either in the government, or in the country. If Ara wasn't dead, he would be better off dead, and sooner rather than later.

"It's my fault," Aunt Gracia said. "If I hadn't put the idea of marrying into your head, Sam would never have made us come here. You would never have met that boy. They had no business taking you with them."

"You didn't put the idea of marrying into my head. I was pregnant," I said.

"Don't be silly," she said.

Ara's father delivered a marriage certificate, hand-lettered, illuminated and signed. Ara and I had been married in St. Gregoire's chapel before we even met. Sammi was fully legal. Ara's mother wanted to see her granddaughter.

"She should have thought of that when Ara was around to care," I said. "Because I don't."

Sammi cried when her grandfather left. She had spent hours ordering him around with hand signals and babbles. I hoped he wouldn't come back. He looked too much like Ara. I had wanted Sammi to be all of Ara, to have nothing of Mama or me. So far, except for a suspicious fullness of her rosebud mouth, she didn't look a bit like him, and I thanked each of my marauding and pillaging crusader ancestors and my Turkish blood, even though, as Varti had put it, sometimes there wasn't a heck of a lot of difference between us visually, Armenian and Turk (blasphemous words uttered only out of earshot of 100% Armenians).

Ara's mother came next, looking small and crumpled, to tell me that I was a punishment from God. Her whole life had been a punishment from God, beginning with the disappearance of her father, to the death marches, to the loss of her sons. Now I was robbing her of her only grandchild.

Sammi wouldn't go to her. She clung to me and screamed.

"Don't blame this one on God," I said. "Blame yourself. You filled Ara with so many of your horror stories that he thought it had happened to him. As long as we keep telling ourselves those stories they keep on winning, because we stop ourselves from living. Sammi will never hear them — not from me, not from you. I'll take her somewhere no one has ever heard of us and our genocide."

She laughed then. In that case, I would have to take Sammi to the ends of the earth, for we inhabited the earth like ghosts.

She left.

"Sosi," Aunt Gracia said. "How can you be so heartless? You don't know what her life has been like, to be the only survivor out of a family of thirteen. Imagine how lonely she has been."

"I don't care what her life has been like. I care what Ara's has been like. And I care that she has destroyed my family."

"I don't recognize you," she said. "You can't go on like this."

Photographs arrived of Mariam the Madonna and the infant enveloped in her radiance. It was clear from the pictures that no one had the least worry about everyone not adoring everyone else. There was a note from Nissim. He had told Mariam that Ara had returned to Jerusalem. He didn't want to spoil her happiness with her new baby.

Aunt Gracia kept the photographs beside her bed. She wanted to go back. The house was big enough. Our babies could grow up together. But I couldn't, for it was always there, the river, mirrored blue light; the kid, trapped, bleating; rocks striking my back as I fled. And then it was Sammi running, Sammi living my life.

The cold November rains began. The skies were gloomy, and the crows were wet. The house was damp, and Sammi wouldn't keep her socks on.

Meri was planning for Christmas. This year we would join in the five-mile procession from Jerusalem to Bethlehem. Sammi would be turning two. She was climbing, babbling. Meri's first memory was at the same age sitting on her father's shoulders, floating on a river of flickering candlelight. As children they were the ultimate Catholics, for they took part in everyone's processions, the Roman Catholic on December 25th, the Orthodox on January 6th, and their own congregation on January 17th. I didn't want to go. I didn't want to have to remember Ara in his navy coat and white scarf, our footprints melting into one another in the sunlight. I didn't want to be seduced by the chants, the incense, and silken lamplight.

Sammi and I played on Mama's carpet, drawing stories out of the blood red and midnight blue, peopling the hills and valleys with cousins who were kind and aunts who took me in out of the cold. I twined a band of prayers around her wrists, a band knit from Mama's tattered memories. We fell asleep together. The rain fell and the turtledoves mourned.

Aunt Gracia found us and had hysterics.

"I know what this is," she said. "It's you getting ready to lie down and die. Go ahead. Just stab me with a knife." She telegrammed Varti to "do something" about me. There was a return telegram that week: "Planning to die? Come to Montreal first."

Aunt Gracia wept.

"First Sammy sees a stork, then he abandons me, and you run off and get married without even telling me. Now when I'm just getting used to it here, you want to run off again. What kind of place is Canada? Who ever heard of Canada?"

"You sent her the telegram."

"I wanted her to come back. I didn't expect you to go running there."

"Varti likes it. She's happy there."

"Of course she's happy there. She's back with her family. They'd be happy in a dungeon together. If you don't want to go to Turkey, we could go to Lebanon. Meri's boys are there. They want her to come. How is Ara going to find you if you're halfway around the world?"

"This is the Middle East," I said. "There hasn't been peace in the Middle East since time began. If it isn't the tribes who live here fighting, it's tribes from somewhere else fighting over us."

Mariam's mother was still convinced that the region was far too barbaric, including the steam baths where people were publicly naked. Girls — whether literate or illiterate; rich or poor; Armenian, Muslim, or Jew — were still being doweried off like so many sets of sheets and so many gold bracelets. All of us, Christian, Muslim, and Jew, were rooted in the Old Testament with its proscriptions of circumcision or stoning for errant women. Too many women left the family courtyard only twice in their lives, at marriage and at death. Tentative gains for women could be lost at a moment's notice.

"Besides," I said, "I don't want Sammi growing up here."

"You grew up here. It didn't hurt you."

I was too much for her; she had no strength left; I was wearing her out; and why wasn't I even the least bit like Mariam? Why didn't I have any of her ability to accept what life gave? I wasn't answering Mariam's letters, either. What was I trying to do, punish Mariam for her happiness?

"Don't blame me," I said. "I never wanted to leave the mountains. It wasn't my idea to come here, either. I was happy playing volleyball. Now Ara's gone, and I'm doing the only thing I can. I'm giving Sammi a new life. What do you expect me to say to Mariam? Sammi's Armenian blood goes back to Noah's ark. Her Turkish blood goes back at least a thousand years. Your ancestors have been in Asia Minor only since the Spanish Inquisition, but Mariam's baby can grow up there, and mine can't. Go live with Mariam. She's your granddaughter. I'm only a niece. An adopted niece. Not even flesh and blood."

She slapped me.

"Don't ever say that to me again. You're my daughter. I know the difference even if you don't."

I didn't. Parents came and went. Disappeared when you least expected it. Mariam was imbedded in her life like moss on rock.

Aunt Gracia stopped speaking to me. I didn't say I was sorry, and I didn't write to Mariam.

Then Aunt Gracia found out that Varti lived in the only part of North America that was French.

"Ha!" Aunt Gracia said. (To Sammi. Not to me.) "I spend all my life avoiding France — and now I'm going to France."

"It's not France," I said. "For heaven's sake, I thought you would be happy — at least it's a place where you can speak the language. I give up. Go where you want. Mariam wants you, Meri wants you... I can take care of myself."

"You. I'm not worried about you. I'm worried about Sammi."

"I can take care of my baby."

"You're both babies. You're taking me away from Sam. How can you take me away? I'll never be able to visit his grave. Who will take care of his grave?"

"Mr. Abhessera will take care of his grave. He's already taking care of his grave. We'll be doing Meri a favour, too. If we leave, she'll move to Beirut to be with her sons. As long as we stay, so will she."

We went to Uncle Samuel's grave to plant a cedar tree — a monument which would endure unto the seventh seventh generation. Sammi tried to pull it out.

I took Sammi to Jaffa to see her grandparents. The sea rippled lemon light and there was ginger and salt in the air. I told Ara's father that I would send pictures, and some day I would send her back. She had a right to know her grandparents.

I was lying. Sammi would grow up in a country that had no massacres, no wars, no genocides. She would speak their language, learn their stories, and play their games. She would know only songs of life. She had a right to know nothing of the history that had consumed her father, nothing of those who had driven him to it: you couldn't know so much about dying and not belong to it. Papa had been wrong when he had said that Mama was afraid to come with us: she had stayed behind because she wanted her dying to end.

# III

## MONTREAL

# CHAPTER 13

I thought it would be a new beginning, but leaving Uncle Samuel was a mistake. For the first time, there was no one to listen to my stories, no one to temper them.

We had begun a tradition when I was small. In the evening when he came home from the shop, he would search me out and tell me the story of his day. He called them stories. It might be a single incident, a simple image of a puppy battling with a stick, or it might be ongoing and complex, the latest chapter in the machinations of the shopkeepers' wives, for instance, who were in an endless competition with each other, particularly over Zaven. They blamed themselves for not recognizing his son-in-law potential when he first appeared on the square, a shy uncertain boy working himself up from answering calls for coffee, to sweeping, to shifting and lifting, to selling, miraculously both unencumbered of an interfering family and, after all these years, as gentle as the first winds of spring. He had also become as stubborn as a mule, refusing to see where his own good lay.

Ami Zaven never told stories himself. It was as if there was no past, and no future. There was only the present: "Who wants to remember? Who wants to worry about what will come tomorrow? It's enough that we have what we have today." I used to imagine sometimes that he and Mama were twins, separated by the chaos of the marches. But I never told him. I never told anyone, not even Mariam. It wasn't a game.

In the beginning, I had no stories, just facts — "Emek lied" — but for Uncle Samuel even a single fact served as inspiration. There were no empty spaces in the art of the Orient, our mosaics, our carpets, filled with colour and shape that kept the eye, the mind, and the heart, busy. This was not a place for a few black lines on white: what was the lie? to whom? about whom? why would one child want to make life miserable for another? did Emek have friends? did he act alone? whom would this lie hurt? There was always a reason for what people did, even if we, with our poor imaginations, couldn't find it. For Aunt Gracia, though, there were no mysteries: people were good or evil, and there weren't enough years in a lifetime for her to understand the foibles of man. In any case, Aunt Gracia never trusted the good. Life was always ready to pounce.

Once, sitting on his grave, recounting the day — Sammi's first tooth, Varti's letter — I felt his hand on my shoulder. I heard his voice, threaded through the silence.

When Ara disappeared, there didn't seem to be anything to say. I went to Uncle Samuel's grave one more time after we decided to leave. I wanted him to understand why we had to go.

At first, being with Varti again was a relief: "If forgetting is what you want, kid," she announced when she met us at the airport, "this is the place. You'll be strangers in a strange land. Nothing here that will remind you of any of your homes, not an echo."

"Including you," I said. "What happened to you? Is this what happens when you fall in love?"

She was transformed, in a brown and white linen suit, pencil-slim skirt, fitted jacket, nylon stockings, and white high-heeled sandals. The long stuffed-under-Joe's-hat hair was gone, replaced by a boyish cap of waves.

"We don't talk about him," she said. "It's the car. Pop's bribe. Bribes never worked when I was a kid, but, hey, we have to grow up sometime. What do you think of my T-Bird with its snazzy V-8 engine, power steering, white-walled tires? Pops is mad about cars. Can you believe it? My very own dad. Nothing like being a prodigal daughter. And this is Sammi. Look at you. What a sweetie. Our very own house kid." Sammi was hiding behind my leg.

Varti stowed our bags in the cavernous trunk of her long, low, peaches-and-cream T-Bird, and helped Aunt Gracia in to the front, propped her up with cushions so she could see over the dashboard, kissed her on the top of her head, and handed us each a bottle of water: "Okay, so there's an echo. Drink up. We freeze in the winter, but we fry in the summer. You can't imagine how excited the parents are that you are here. Ma is already looking at patterns for little girls. In fact, she's got heaps of dresses that she couldn't get me to wear. Poor Ma. Now I actually get a kick out of playing dress-up. You, too, Sosi, she's got plans for you. I told her that you weren't much better than me. And if you think I'm chatty, wait till you meet Dad."

Aunt Gracia reached across to pat Varti's hand: "Thank you, Varti. You have always been so thoughtful. I don't think I ever thanked you."

"Me? Thoughtful? You don't ever have to thank me, Aunt G. Promise me you won't thank me. Remember Uncle Samuel, balance and trade. How was the trip? Nothing like airplanes, I tell you. Give me an airplane any day. I think I was meant to be a pilot. What did you think? Wasn't it great?"

"No," Aunt Gracia said.

Air travel made no sense at all to Aunt Gracia. What was wrong with travelling the way God intended, on land, slow enough to see where you were going, and able to do something about it if the car broke down or the camel got stubborn? She kept herself awake from take-off to landing, following the clouds, the sky, the ocean below. It was only as we drove from the airport, past farms and church spires in the distance, that she fell asleep. She woke up just as we drove into the centre of the city. "Ah. Paris," she said. "Why didn't you say so?"

"Not Paris, Aunt Gracia," Varti said. "Montreal, rich man's substitute, only three-story walk-up flats instead of six." But Aunt Gracia had already fallen back asleep.

There were only two other cars on the street. Children hopscotching, skipping, and shooting each other down with finger pistols moved to let us through. "And there," she said, as the car drew up to a sidewalk in the centre of a street that was a canyon of three-story greystone row housing and dark-leafed trees, "is my pair of parents. Aren't they cute?"

Varti's pair of parents stood at attention, Mrs. Adoian (Ma, Mom, Momsy) in a neat, cool, eyelet shirtwaist dress and perfectly waved hair. "Don't be fooled," Varti said. "Beneath that high fashion exterior beats a heart of pure, old-fashioned mom." Mr. Adoian (Pa, Pops, Dad, Dadsy, short, bald, chubby, with Ami's magnificent eyebrows) was bowing to Aunt Gracia: "Thank you for sending our daughter home. Thank you for coming. Joe, rest his soul, was a nice boy — we shouldn't have been so mean to him. Imagine, a successful teacher going back to the old country — who goes back to the old country? Nobody. And look what happens. He leaves her a widow, and frankly, if he had been good for her, would she be so afraid to marry again? So we discussed it, Fimi and I — you will call us Fimi and Chris — when you live in the same house, how can you be formal? We said to Varti, what are they going to do in Jerusalem? In the '20s and '30s, we were two families living here, but since the war, things have picked up. The store supports us — nobody buys milk on credit these days — and to tell you the truth, since we bought the building, the rent from the other two apartments could support us. In our apartment, eight rooms, we said to Varti, 'Only the three of us, it's criminal.'"

He was helping Aunt Gracia up the steps to the second-floor apartment. Aunt Gracia stood in the hallway dwarfed by ten-foot ceilings and eight-foot oak doors.

They had put us in the double room in the front with a large window looking down onto the street, a bed-sitting room with a chintz sofa bed and chairs. The smaller room in the back closed off with frosted glass doors. Aunt Gracia crumpled onto the bed. Sammi flopped down beside her and instantly fell asleep.

"Are you okay?" I said.

"Of course," she said. "Your uncle was French. And you especially should be grateful. It was because of our name that your grandfather trusted him. He wouldn't have let anyone with a Turkish name take him in with your mother, an Armenian orphan, along. Mind you, most of the shopkeepers would have helped him out. We're not all heartless, no matter what our names are. Look how they helped Zaven."

She fell asleep talking. I wasn't used to Aunt Gracia having so many good things to say about people.

"Well, pipsqueak?" Varti said. "How is she doing?" We were sitting on the front landing so she could have a cigarette. Chris and Fimi still didn't know that their prodigal daughter smoked which, even Varti had to admit, was either denial or a miracle.

"Aunt Gracia seems to have decided that she can like it here because it's France. As long as she never figures out that this is Canada, we're okay. What about you? You look like you're having fun."

"Mostly, I guess. I'd forgotten that Mom and Dad were so cute. Aunt Gracia was right, though — you don't take your whole heart with you. It's weird. My friends have no idea what to talk to me about. It's like I've been on the moon for ten years, not one experience in common. Almost a whole decade, pouf, gone. And you know what? You never know what you're going to miss, like the Judean Hills in the moonlight. And do you know what else? I miss being in a country where everyone has a purpose. Even though none of it was ever my purpose."

A person just never knew, she said, what was going to jump up and grab you.

Wasn't life just the damnedest?

"And," she added, "I wouldn't mention 'my man' in front of that pair of parents. It's a bit of a sore point. I'm still trying to forgive them."

She had expected her parents to be thrilled with her short, dark, handsome Christian guy. She had to admit to naiveté, the last thing she ever thought she'd be able to accuse herself of. After living in the kaleidoscope of the world's three major religions in their countless variations — Armenian Orthodox, Greek Orthodox, Russian Orthodox; Egyptian Coptic and Ethiopian Coptic; East Indian Jews, Ethiopian Jews, Kurdish Jews, European Jews, and North African Jews; Roman Catholics and Armenian Catholics; Lutherans and Presbyterians and Baptists and Methodists; Sunni Muslims and Shia Muslims; black Christians, Arab Christians and white Christians; Gregorian Armenians, Catholic Armenians and Protestant Armenians — all she had thought about was that he was Christian. She had barely noticed his colour until she saw the shock on her father's face. Patrick had broken it off. This was too much of a reminder of the rest of his life. He had fought for "his" country, but he couldn't go to "their" universities or rent "their" apartments. He was the first to admit, though, that he could work anywhere in the country from sea to shining sea. As long as it was on a train.

Nothing personal, he said, but he didn't want to have to fight battles during Sunday dinner with the in-laws, too.

"All of which is to say," she said, "that I can devote myself entirely to you guys. Thank god you're here. Even I need to

be reminded sometimes that I haven't been on the moon for
ten years."

We went for Sunday outings in Varti's peaches-and-
cream T-Bird, the windows down, Varti's hand catching the
wind. We laughed. So far from anything we had known, loved,
feared, and left behind. We drove north into pine and spruce
forests, past glittering lakes, or up along the shore of the St.
Lawrence River through villages with brightly painted houses,
soft yellows and blues. And always there were those church
spires, glittering in the distance above the trees, the one solid
rock-like presence in humble villages of wood. The villages,
farms, homes, were open. Nothing was designed to close up
against night marauders. They could be entered at any point.
Where was the fear? The tribal battles?

"Don't get carried away," Varti said. "This is a French
and Roman Catholic province, and our despotic premier won't
let you forget it. We're a banana republic. The premier is a
law unto himself. He can get you thrown into jail. He can
have your taxes doubled. One word, and he can get the pulp
and paper companies to double their prices. Why do you think
the newspapers support him? So they can afford to keep on
operating. And we've voted him in for fifteen years straight.
Never underestimate the power of the vote."

"But no one is killing anyone over religion."

"True. You have a point. Maybe I complain too much.
You're right. You made the right decision. At least we can all
look forward to growing old."

"It wasn't a decision. It was desperation."

"Desperation counts. So far, I'd say you have a record
of fine escaping instincts."


Aunt Gracia in "that French country" was now entirely
amenable and agreeable. It was up to me now, she said, it was
out of her hands. (Or, as Aisha Hanim would have put it,

*inshallah.*) She was constantly amazed and interested, writing notes to Ara's parents (someone had to behave in a civilized manner), and fat letters in flowing French to Aimée (the most wonderful daughter-in-law a mother could wish for). In Aunt Gracia's letters, our raucous three-story row house neighbourhood had the greystone elegance of Paris, complete with balconies above, below, and across, that Aunt Gracia remembered from her one (disastrous) visit. There were no donkeys roaming the streets, no camels or goats. Women smoked, wore lipstick and hats; arranged marriages and dowries were unheard of; there were French newspapers; there was a steam bath; there were streetcars.

She took to the streets. Her world had become a giant market square. She disappeared for hours at a time, returning with life histories of mailmen and mothers, carpenters and car mechanics, storekeepers and stonemasons, nurses and nuns. They were French, they were English, they were Irish, they were Chinese. They were Italian, Jewish, and Greek. She had been in a streetcar, on a park bench, in a church, or at a garage. She was invited in for *biscotti*, bowls of noodles, and cups of tea. She had mapped the city. We were in the immigrant centre three blocks west of the St. Lawrence Street dividing line (English: west; French: east). Following St. Lawrence Street south to the St. Lawrence River was Chinatown, the banks, the factories, the wharves. Cross streets led west to department stores and, if you walked far enough, to a world of the English with front lawns and children in school uniforms. But only ten minutes' walk from us, blessedly green, blessedly cool, was Mount Royal and an enormous park. Aunt Gracia napped under the trees.

While Sammi constructed giant church spires that crumbled in the sandbox or waded in the paddling pool, I worried: "At least you could tell me where you're going. What if something happens to you?"

"How can I tell you if I don't know?"

"Boy," Varti said, "for a woman who spent her life a captive of courtyards, she certainly has busted loose."

"Don't listen to Aunt Gracia — she was only captive when it suited her. She wasn't locked away in a mountain village, you know."

"It doesn't matter. She's acting weird. I hope this isn't the calm before some kind of storm."

Aunt Gracia had brought her space with her. She had arrived fully developed, prominent on the foreground, moving through time and light as if it was her right, yet more and more I needed to know that when I stood in the sun, shadows fell, when I sat on a bench, it was filled. I needed to know that the greystone and red brick of this city was as true as the golden limestone of Jerusalem, as the whitewashed walls of our seaside city, of my mountain village. My village that was a dream.

I walked through Aunt Gracia's city with Sammi, trying to see what Aunt Gracia saw, trying to escape the walls, seeking familiarity in a leaf, a shadow, a cloud. But the river was quick and cold, the sky pale, distant, and the thick green of the trees drained the light out of the sky. The tawny coats of our hooded crows had become raven black, and their cry harsh. Strident. Defiant.

On rainy days, we retreated inside shops on St. Lawrence Street or Mount Royal Avenue, a jumble of languages, a jumble of goods: fabric shops, stacked to the ceiling with bolts of cottons and wools, boxes of buttons, zippers, and threads; poultry shops stacked with cages of live chickens and geese; fur shops with sample pelts, mink, beaver, otter, fox; vegetable shops, sad affairs of carrots and celery and potatoes and cabbage and onions, not a zucchini or eggplant in sight, no fresh parsley, no fresh herbs. Restaurants served up weak, watery coffee, and tea-bag tea.

Sometimes we rode the streetcar instead, the grey and green city a blur behind raindrops pelting down the glass. We got off to explore the department stores, Ali Baba's caves of treasures, swept in by revolving brass doors and floated up on escalators or in elevators with white-gloved elevator girls. There were forests of hanging racks that could be wandered through at will, that could hide a child and dress a dozen villages. Backless dresses and circle skirts, see-through blouses and strapless bathing suits. Restrooms where Sammi could nap on my lap. Soda bars. Restaurants. Magical machines controlled by djinn, who, we decided, lived inside the switches: electric irons, electric floor polishers, and electric mixers; vacuum cleaners, automatic washers and automatic dryers, transistor radios. Television. Moving pictures in a box.

I wanted money. Aunt Gracia and I knew nothing about money. It had always been Uncle Samuel's affair. Maurice was sending money from Turkey. Varti and I exchanged it at her bank, a white-pillared temple with the nobility of the Grecian ruins in Turkey. Our money was piling up in a drawer in Aunt Gracia's room, bills of happy colours, blue, and green, and orange. Chris and Fimi wouldn't take any of it. The days were long past when boarders were needed to help pay the rent. Now they had the pleasure of being hosts to their friends. We could put our money into savings bonds, or at least open an account at a bank. We could make money with our money, through no effort of our own. Canada would pay us to use our money.

A pile of the money disappeared one day. My aunt, who had never seen any reason to change or add to her own home other than to repair or replace a cushion for the sitting room now and then (the carpets had been her mother's, the tapestries had been in the family for generations, even the pots of roses and the wisteria had a history), came home with an electric kettle, then an electric coffee pot, a waffle iron, an electric frying pan, surprises for Fimi and Chris, she said, a way to make their lives easier after twelve- or fifteen-hour days at the store. The kitchen, according to Sammi, was now full of djinn, and she wasn't convinced that they knew their places. "They are minor djinn," Aunt Gracia said. "Always well behaved. Well brought up. Or they get sent to their rooms."

One afternoon, just after Aunt Gracia and I had dashed onto the back balcony to rescue the sheets from the rain, she was struck by guilt. Washing day was the one day of the week that she and Aisha Hanim had both hated, dragging out the big kettles, heating up the water, rubbing and wringing the sheets. There were villages in Turkey where clothes were still beaten against the rocks in the river and laid out on the grass to dry. All those years she had tortured Aisha Hanim with the wash.

Yet even Fimi's electric wringer washer took an entire day, coaxing it out of the corner on squeaking wheels and setting up in the middle of the kitchen, filling it with water by a hose connected to the kitchen tap, setting up tubs for rinsing. She and I had taken on the task, and at first this electric washer had seemed better. But she looked at the washer one rainy morning, and the pile of clothes on the floor: "Enough," she said.

A week later, Chris and Fimi came back from the shop to find Aunt Gracia in the furnace room behind the kitchen explaining the complexity of washing and drying djinn to Sammi, the water djinni (hot or cold), the rubbing djinni, the wringing djinni, the rinsing and spinning djinni. The drying djinni with the hot breath of summer would do our bidding, day or night, rain, snow, or shine. Chris thought it might be easier to explain electricity. Aunt Gracia had plans to ship sets to Aimée, to Mariam, and to Aisha Hanim.

Varti was getting nervous. Everyone was happy except me: Sammi had a multitude of laps; Fimi had a surrogate grandchild; Chris had his daughter, his car fanatic buddy; Aunt Gracia was roaming the streets; and I was acting weird. Shut up like a clam. Strung tighter than a drum. I was going to snap. She had seen it happen. She hadn't brought me here for peace and safety just to have me melt down.

I had been forcing Varti to take pictures of me with Sammi. I had been sending snapshots of us to Aisha Hanim, to Father Hovanissian, to Meri, with notes on the backs of the photos explaining where we were and who we were with, so that one day Sammi would be able to search herself out, gather in the fragments, reclaim certainty from those who had held the truth of her in their hands. For I was all uncertainty, waking each morning at dawn searching the silence, fighting for breath, fighting against panic.

"I'm fine," I said.

"You're not fine. You're all stressed out. I had a University of Montreal professor in my cab the other day, the inventor of stress, though he said he was the discoverer, as if it needed to be discovered, telling me that I need a stress-free job. Mind you, he did admit that maybe I didn't find it as stressful as he would. Each to his own stress, I say. And here all this time you and I thought it was only starvation and childbirth and the desert sun that did you in. But no. We can stay home, and just quietly die. And you had better not. I thought Aunt Gracia would be the tough one, but it's you."

Even Aunt Gracia was getting worried.

"Don't make the mistake I did, Sosi," she said.

All her problems, she said, had been her own doing. Growing up in the home she had been born in, marriage to Uncle Samuel, ever sunny and sweet-natured, had been a charmed life. All her stress had been from trying to manage other people's lives, and ultimately, we had proved unmanageable, Maurice marrying Aimée, a perfectly lovely woman, a good mother, and a good aunt to me: it couldn't have been easy giving up her family and country to go to a mother-in-law so ridiculously protective of her son. Now she couldn't think of what on earth she was trying to protect him from.

And as if that wasn't bad enough, I had come along, and she had started all over again. Yet the two of us, Maurice and I, had done what we were going to do anyway.

And here she was, living a life beyond her imagination. Without Sam.

"He'd have been proud of you," I said.

"I don't want him to be proud," she said. "I want him to be here."

I missed him beyond words.

I missed Ara, too. I had escaped him, anything that reminded me of him, and now I missed him. I missed him singing to Sammi, I missed his mad history lessons, I missed stirring honey into his morning yoghurt, and I missed sleeping curled around his back. I missed him in the photographs.

Summer had ended. It was only September, the best of summer in southern Turkey and Jerusalem, a softening of the summer heat, but here there was a crispness in the night air. Leaves fell, garnet and gold rustling like rain. I tried to see in the colours lying at our feet the garnets and rubies that Ara had promised Sammi as a baby.

# CHAPTER 14

It wasn't long before the streets were long geometric strips of grey and black, dull concrete sidewalks, greystone facades, winding black iron staircases. The miniature gardens had been bronzed by frost. The trees lost their leaves and stood, stark. Bereft. Grey and brown sparrows chattered, worrying the tall branches.

Varti had adapted to the theme in a black tweed suit, camel-hair coat, black kid leather gloves, black fur-trimmed overshoes, layers of wool felt and woolly socks in the boots instead of shoes, and warm woolen pink bloomers. No one had to know about the unsexy bloomers and the socks. This was a show, a performance. The book was judged by its cover.

Varti's hours in the taxi had grown longer, but not because she was making more money. She was busy with the Turkish Armenians who had arrived with holiday visas to escape a wave of random attacks. They were overstaying their visas, and the government was getting ready to deport them. They were terrified of going back. In 1915, the massacres had been set in motion by government decree. This time, it was the neighbours. Not all, not organized, but enough. A few dead were too many dead. The friends who warned them or hid them weren't enough to make up for the ones who hunted.

She was angry with me. I wouldn't help, and it was obvious to anyone with half a brain, let alone half a heart, that I was the best person for the job.

"Me?" I said. "Why?"

"Turkish, dimwit. Your language. Number one speak. Your country. A common enemy. Shared misery."

"Some people think Mama should have thrown herself down a well rather than marry a Turk. I don't know how much we'll have in common when they find out I have a Turkish father," I said. "Can't I share my misery when I'm less miserable?"

Aunt Gracia volunteered. Aunt Gracia's letters home had changed. The recipes she had made thousands of times at home weren't working: lamb soup wasn't lamb soup when only beef was available, and there was no substitute at all for eggplant. Varti had warned her that we would have to bring a jar of yoghurt starter, but it had never occurred to her that she would have to bring a whole garden as well. Not only that, but the grandmothers on the park benches were an inexhaustible source of lore, and she now knew that "this French country" was indeed a country, a country within a country, with laws, customs, and idiosyncrasies of its own based on French common law, while the rest of Canada, based on English common law, was entirely different. They spit, these grandmothers, on the cavalcade of hundreds of flower-laden cars mourning the premier's death, while they feared the priests who thundered damnation from the pulpits and threatened them in the confessionals. Any less than a baby a year was a denial of their husbands, a denial of God, and a denial of the French fact: the English had conquered in 1765, but they would be outnumbered one day. They would lose by demographics.

Yet the birthing rooms were death chambers. In the Catholic hospitals, with a difficult birth, it was God's will that the baby should live; mother had already had her life. And no matter what Varti had said about women not being dowered off, the law still allowed girls to be married at twelve and their brothers at fourteen.

Their grandchildren were beginning to rebel, quietly, staying away from church. What you didn't hear couldn't affect you.

And we, Aunt Gracia pronounced, dared to call Turkey backward.

Varti graciously refrained from reminding her that there was something a tad "backward" about Armenians having to flee Turkey still, now, in the '50s because Aunt Gracia's help was invaluable. She was translating, and Varti was going to government offices. Chris had a new purpose: he could help set up other people in shops to sell canned salmon and alphabet soup. I had given orders that I wasn't to be mentioned at all. No one needed to know that I had come from Turkey. I would simply be the mother of the child who chattered all the time: *"Quels beaux yeux bleus!"* and "Okey-doke," and "Where is everybody?" and "Can I go with Varti in the T-Bird all the time if I promise to be quiet?"

With these new Armenians who spoke Armenian and Turkish, both languages were blossoming. Even Fimi, Varti's mother, fluent in Armenian when Chris had searched her out in New York out of a sudden loneliness for a stolen past, and too embarrassed by the remnants of almost thirty years of disuse to speak it at all, was in the flush of rediscovery. Words she had no idea she had ever known were popping up.

I didn't want Sammi speaking Armenian or Turkish. I wanted her to be an ordinary child.

Varti laughed. It was very close to her hysterical desert laugh: "Which 'ordinary' are you talking about?" she said. "French like the province? English like the country? If you're Irish or

Chinese or Jewish or Black, you can't rent an apartment or go to a restaurant outside your neighbourhood, and if you're French, no one understands a word you say the second you leave the province. Relax, Sos. Around here everybody is like everybody else because they're not like everybody else. Mind you, some people are too much not like everyone else."

She was worn out from working against the clock. Aunt Gracia and I had been easy. We had been sponsored as family, but there was a limit to how many you could add to the roster before suspicions were raised.

Driving taxi was a break, especially, for her, at night. She liked watching the city change to sapphire twilight, to streetlamps and neon nightlife. But she hated coming home to silence. If I had fallen asleep on the couch listening to "Country Hoedown" or "Our Miss Brooks" on the radio after putting Sammi to sleep, she would shake me awake. She envied me having Sammi. She had never been enlisted in so many hide-and-seek games by her own personal house kid. She and Joe probably should have had children; at least she would have something of his other than guilt. She wasn't likely to have children now. Patrick had been her last chance.

She was trying not to feel sorry for herself. You couldn't hate a guy for not wanting to make his future children's lives miserable. Helping other people get over their traumas wasn't always as uplifting as it was cracked up to be. We needed to get out, she said: she was overwhelmed by man's inhumanity to man, and I was moping over Ara, whether I wanted to admit it or not. There was a whole world out there. Department stores were just the beginning. We were in one of the swingingest cities of the world, yet we were living like willing inmates of a monastery. Every Tom, Dick, and Harry fresh off trains from Chicago, New York, Toronto, Ottawa, lurid newspaper headlines tucked under their arms, headed first for the "hot spots." She knew them all, the uptown clubs for the blue-eyed unaccented ones, and the downtown clubs for all the others. She could get us into either, but the downtown clubs with all the unacceptables — Blacks, Italians, the Irish, the Jews — were more fun.

"*Night* clubs?" Aunt Gracia said. In Turkey, concerts, volleyball, anything respectable, was in the afternoon. After dark, you were home and accounted for.

"Music clubs," Varti said. "Music is relaxing."

"Wow," I said. This was Varti's word. "A whole new world." I was ready for a new world. I was ready for one of those backless dresses, a circle skirt. Or possibly a sheath. I tried to imagine feeling like a woman and not like a mom.

"Not a chance," Varti said. She hadn't paid enough attention the first time. I was young and defenseless, and if anyone touched me, she would cut off his hands. In fact, maybe this was a bad idea. She knew those guys, the musicians; Tom, Dick, and Harry; the rowdy Irish boys from the wrong side of the tracks who seemed to have a choice of only two career paths, cops or robbers. They would be all over me, new kid on the block.

They weren't all over me, even though we were a matched set, demure in our straight black wool skirts, white silk blouses, and velvet chokers. They were all over her, back on the scene. Joe, a high school teacher, had been a jazz fanatic, and Varti had caught the bug. Joe used to take a turntable and records to his classes. Somehow jazz was useful in teaching math. Musicians were mathematicians, according to Joe, and jazz musicians, with all that syncopation and double rhythms, were the top of the heap: they could do more with one beat than a physicist could do with an atom.

Varti ordered my drink (Coke), wouldn't let me try her cigarettes, and told "the boys" that I was sixteen. Some of the boys had lovely bums and capable hands, and some of them didn't remind me of Ara at all. They were happy. I watched them, joking, laughing, comfortable with their cigarettes, their drinks, and their lives.

"That wasn't so bad," Varti said. "Never heard the word 'visa' once. I feel better, how about you?"

"Pretty good," I said.

We did it again, and it felt even better. "The boys" said one drink wouldn't hurt me. Varti approved crème de menthe, green, pretty. I became very good at sitting in my corner watching those lovely bums and delicious hands and drinking quietly, so no one noticed what or how many I had — I had my own money, after all, pretty green and blue bills from Aunt Gracia's drawer. I tried all the drinks, the innocent ones, rum and Coke, vodka and orange juice, Bloody Marys. I tipped generously so the bar-tender wouldn't rat on me. I moved on to martinis, with pale olive and without. I learned that not all martinis are equal. I learned to smoke. It added a *je ne sais quoi* to the tilt of a martini glass.

I settled finally on gin and tonic as my drink of choice, no colour, no olive, all taste and light, a mountain tang with a touch of Mediterranean sultry. Varti was faithful to Scotch, a solid desert drink. A touch of burn.

Eventually, word got out that I wasn't sixteen, and that I was a mother, to boot. Varti lost credibility. She let her guard down. We both got drunk. We both got "taken advantage of." We sat in the kitchen over coffee at dawn; Varti diagnosed that the time for diaphragms had arrived.

"Does it count as 'taken advantage of,'" I said, "if we like it?"

"Not on your life," she said. "But it doesn't keep you from getting pregnant, either."

"Oh, yeah," I said. "That's right."

"There's something wrong with this picture," Varti said. "Montreal is probably the most sinful city on the continent. I shouldn't have brought you here. I'm corrupting you. I'm a widow. An old widow. I'm thirty-two, for god's sake. You're a twenty-year-old wife and mother."

"What about fun?" I said. "Remember fun? You're not going to quit just when I'm learning to have fun, are you? Am I supposed to be on the shelf for the rest of my life just because my daughter's father ran off to play Christians and Romans?"

"Ara," she said. "His name is Ara."

"Thank you. And I'm his widow. We are both widows, thank you very much."

"You don't know that."

But I knew that. I knew that every night, and I knew it every morning. I knew it each time Sammi called for *Baba*. She hadn't forgotten yet, thanks to Aunt Gracia who had been developing an interest in photographs and seemed to think that going through pictures with Sammi to identify her family, past and present, was a valid game.

"You know what, pipsqueak?" Varti said. "I've figured it out. We're always in the wrong fairy tale, you and I. We don't seem to know how to identify stay-at-home princes, you know, guys who aren't determined to run off to carve out new kingdoms or battle dragons."

"Right," I said. "Joe carting you off to Israel, and Ara tramping through Turkey searching out persecuted Armenians. I could have stuck to the name Zeyneb and let Aunt Gracia marry me off to Nissim and Mrs. Behar. It could be me writing glowing letters about a baby boy and his adorable chubby feet just like Nissim's."

"Forget it, kid," Varti said. "That's Mariam's fairy tale. You can't wish yourself into being a different princess. Neither of us can, I guess."

She poured more coffee from the electric coffee pot. There was something to be said for that electric coffeepot: it never bubbled over from drunken inattention. That enterprising djinni did his job. She considered whether we ought to take up the Armenian women on their offers of cousins in Turkey. At least we would get two more of them out of the country.

"I was thinking more along the lines of a nice Canadian boy," I said. "Someone good with his hands."

She laughed. She thought I was developing a sense of humour.

Sammi woke me up with conversations about my nose and the dog and that kid last summer who wouldn't let her go down the slide. She ran through her whole vocabulary waking me up. I had discovered hangovers. I got up and scrubbed floors. I didn't feel as guilty when I scrubbed floors. Sammi thought I was playing. I was at her level.

Aunt Gracia, forced indoors by blustery winds and stray snowflakes, had discovered movie theatres and afternoon movies, and now she knew that nightclubs were an excuse for whiskey and cigarettes and guns and sex. Good girls, even in the movies, didn't go to nightclubs. Good girls stayed home, cooked, worried about the children, and waited for their men. Good girls, it seemed, were universal.

But it was getting too cold to go out.

"I've been thinking," she said one evening as Sammi and I were sitting on the bed with her. Sometimes I didn't take Sammi back to bed with me, I just crawled in with both of them. "If Chris and Fimi won't take any money, we could buy them a gift. A real gift. A television." She had it all worked out: we would all stay home together, and Varti and I wouldn't be running off all hours of the night, putting ourselves in danger in nightclubs that were owned by the Mafia who, everyone knew, regularly had people shot. Including by accident.

"Sure," I said. Maybe Aunt Gracia was right. Maybe I didn't want to be a bad girl. "But they're photographs, you know, those moving pictures in a box."

"Don't be silly," she said.

Chris and Varti, the gadget men, were all for it, but Fimi, during quiet moments at the cash register, took out her stacks of *Maclean's* and *Saturday Night* magazines, and she knew that television was destroying family life. Next we would be buying TV tables and eating in front of the television instead of having conversations like civilized people. Teachers who came into the store complained that children weren't doing their homework, and the nuns complained that television was replacing the churches. Not that any of us went to church. Even Aunt Gracia refused invitations to go to neighbourhood synagogues, humbly tucked into street corners; the European Jews here were different, she said. They spoke Yiddish. She spoke Ladino. Their chicken soup was wrong. She had more in common with Varti's Armenians.

So now the television sat, big and square, in the corner of the living room. It was, I had to admit, a pretty good substitute for gin, though it would have been a lot nicer with gin, and it was good for Sammi's and my English. We adopted TVisms: "Oh, really?" "Now cut that out!" "Hey, wait a minute!" Varti didn't need to wake me when she came home late, and she was ahead of the pack with their patter. She knew why the ref was wrong on the offside call; she had seen the interview with Canada's Sweetheart, that plucky sixteen-year-old girl who had swum Lake Ontario; she had seen those pitiful kids done in by a summer mosquito, doomed to life in the iron lung; she supported Prime Minister Diefenbaker's call to end the death penalty. She knew the Wayne and Shuster jokes.

Varti became a TV addict. Snuggling down with the house kid under the covers and watching television on a snowy wintry night was just the ticket. Now she was the one who fell asleep on the living room couch. Television would have been enough for me, too, if it had been in Turkish once in a while. Sometimes I felt like every day was a language lesson, and I didn't want any more lessons. The only thing that marred a winter's evening for her was running out of popcorn (we didn't: Chris brought it home from the store) or worrying about having to dig out the car in the morning. (She didn't have to. Sammi and I dug out the car. We loved snow, soft fluffy snow, blowing snow, and hard-packed crunchy snow. We were a street event. Even the horse delivering the morning milk stopped to take a look.)

Now when I did manage to inveigle Varti out, for some reason (no reason I could figure out), she had rules: we had to be home before either of us had had too much to drink; we would not sleep with anyone until her source had managed to smuggle "the pill" in from across the line; there were to be no telltale cigarette butts left in the guest ashtrays which were, after all, there for decoration, souvenirs from Princess Elizabeth's visit and a Coke salesman.

Then a prince landed on our doorstep, a one-armed Armenian with red hair, freckles, brown eyes, and a shy smile. Our mailman. Aunt Gracia brought him inside like a trophy: Armenians turned up when you least expected them, just as I had appeared, she said, a frightened, angry six-year-old convinced that all the Armenians were dead. Sammi stared. I stared. After a life surrounded by dark-haired everyone, he was a surprise, a flaming maple in a dark forest.

His name was Sean Dolabjian.

"Uh, look, you guys." He talked like Varti. "Don't get the wrong idea. The only thing really Armenian about me is my name. Just my name. My last name, actually."

His father Nick (formerly Neshan) had been among a group of orphans brought to Georgetown, Ontario from Syria after the genocide, a "Georgetown boy." He had been farmed out with an Irish tobacco farmer so that the ten daughters could have a break from planting tobacco, transplanting tobacco, and picking tobacco. It turned out that all ten daughters liked being out with sunrises and nippy air. And tobacco. Besides, he was so young, so thin, so sad. And so hungry. They sneaked him extra food from their plates. They let him sleep in. He grew up to marry one of the farmer's daughters. Now he was the farmer. He listened to hockey on the radio on Saturday nights, he curled, he teased his

redheaded Irish-tempered wife with Black Donnelly jokes,
he had six redheaded children himself (Sean was the only son),
and he never spoke of his Armenian past. It was as if he had
been born eleven years old on that farm. When there was
talk of first memories, his was being picked up in a wagon
and having a horsehair blanket thrown over him because, "the
saints be with us," they'd sent him out "as though they
expected the angels to keep him warm."

Sean Dolabjian had a mail route to finish.

Fimi was speechless, and not only because of this
Armenian on the doorstep, but because on this morning of
all mornings — the first time in years — she was home with a
cold. Wasn't this a sign from God? And add into this that
Chris had been a Georgetown boy, too.

"You'll have to come back," she said. "My husband will
want to meet you."

"Absolutely," Varti said. She was home this morning, as
well, though it was less unusual: we had broken the rule. She
had a hangover. She would be doing the afternoon and evening
shift in the cab. "We have to add you to our collection."

He blushed.

The next morning, Fimi, grateful for her cold, was
waiting for the mail. Aunt Gracia and Sammi were waiting,
too, watching action from the front window. They were
waiting for the snow blowers to shoot the snow into piles on
the street. Next after streetcars, Sammi was particularly fond
of the snow blowers.

Fimi invited Sean in. Our home was his home.

"It's against the rules, ma'am," he said. "You know all
the postman jokes. And then there's that old movie, *The
Postman Always Rings Twice.* You can't be too careful, ma'am."

Varti was just getting up.

"Don't fight it, kid." She was wearing a silk robe, one of
the watery silks that Ara had sent. Aunt Gracia had given it

to Fimi, who had turned it into a robe for Varti: the colour matched her car. "This is Oriental hospitality. Don't even bother."

He blushed again.

"You don't have to blush around me," Varti said. "You're too young and sweet for me."

"No one who was overseas for four years is young," he said. "No matter what their age."

"Sorry, kid," she said. "It's my mouth. It says things before I think them."

"Mine doesn't," he said. "Ma'am."

He was angry. He left. Fimi had just poured coffee. She was angry.

"For Pete's sake," Varti said. "He's just the postman. What on earth would we have in common, me a city widow, and him, a one-armed farm kid who walks all day? Besides, he's more Sosi's age, and Aunt Gracia saw him first."

"He's a nice boy," Aunt Gracia piped up. "Sammi likes him."

It was true. She did.

But it was Fimi's home. She didn't go to the store now, until after the mail was delivered. She was reeling Sean in with tidbits about his Armenian ancestry. Tea and *lahmajoon*, hand-sized pizzas laced with thyme and olive oil, were timed for the mail deliveries, and while she patted them out, she discussed with herself whether telling Sean that Varti had made them for him would be a sin. Lying about a daughter's cooking prowess was, it seemed, also universal.

It kept on snowing, fat, fluffy snowflakes drifting out of a white sky, frosting the trees, sculpting a monochrome world of whites. The silence was as clear as a colour. It was easier not to think about Ara when it snowed, not to wonder if he was still alive and which prison he might be in, and whether Aisha Hanim would run into him in the street huddled against a wall. Ara wasn't in any of my snow memories, not the snow that settled the world with white expectation and allowed a belief in new beginnings.

It was even easier not to think about Ara when I drowned him in gin. I sneaked out of the house before Varti got back and after the others had gone to bed, and particularly on the nights that Sammi chose to fall asleep with Aunt Gracia. I left my coat and boots hanging in the hallway so no one would suspect. I took one of Varti's coats from her closet, and borrowed a pair of her boots.

I drowned him good. I floated on the surface, buoyed by bubbles and the reflected light of a mountain dawn. I found a drummer, fell for his rhythms, for his shoulders, for his workingman hands. For the light of future in his grey eyes. I wanted to get pregnant. I wanted two little bodies snuggling up against me at night. I wanted a father for Sammi. What better reason could there be to go to the club than finding a father for your daughter?

But Varti was waiting up for me one night, curled up in front of the test pattern on the television. Someone had spilled the beans. She knew all about my drummer. "I haven't been paying enough attention," she said. "You're on the rebound here. You're not supposed to fall for those guys. Believe me, the future you see in his eyes isn't you. Relax. You've got your whole life ahead of you."

"That's what I'm worried about," I said.

That night, Ara appeared in a dream, finally, accusing, confused. Why couldn't I stay put? Why was I making it so hard for him to find me?

"What business does Ara have haunting you?" Varti said. "His father is the great promoter of escape, except, of course, escaping with the grandchildren violates some ancient hormonal code. No wonder you feel guilty. You've got the curses of all the grandparents of the ages on your shoulders. Come to think of it, though, maybe you're just feeling sexy. I should have kept us home in the nunnery. We've both been activated. Women get sexier as they get older — just ask me. Mind you, you're not exactly old. You're just a kid. With an old life.

"We've got to find a way to keep you out of trouble," she said. "Look at me. Too tired to get into trouble. You should be helping me out with the Armenians, you know. It would put things into perspective for you."

I needed to get out of the house, she said. I needed to be independent and overtired. It wasn't as though there weren't plenty of people ready to help with Sammi, especially with Aunt Gracia trapped inside all day, and not above using Sammi as bait. Sean was already carrying her around on his shoulders. He wouldn't have been the first man to fall in love with a woman because of her child.

"There's a problem there," I said. "Your mother has him staked out for you."

"Never mind," she said. "Ma will recover. It will give her hope. I'll take the next one who lands on the doorstep. Aunt Gracia will win — that'll be tough — but how can you fight off a kid? Another reason Joe and I should have had some. What was I thinking?"

We had a plan. Since I had exhibited expert driving abilities, albeit in a country of mad drivers on the opposite side of the road, I would get my licence and help out with the taxi. We would double Chris's investment. Two days later, Varti nixed it. I was too young and inexperienced. I couldn't be trusted not to park the car and go in with Tom, Dick, or Harry for a drink. Cabbies tougher than me succumbed to the temptation of free drinks. People liked to drink with their taxi drivers. It made them feel like they were slumming, and there was a haunted *je ne sais quoi* about me that they wouldn't be able to resist.

Sean got me a job in a factory. A safe, indoor job, no training required. Sean knew all the factories in the neighbourhood. He walked me to work. He commiserated because he knew I'd rather be doing Varti's job. He understood the need for freedom. He missed the farm. He missed tinkering with machines. He wasn't needed on the farm. There were two other perfectly handy two-handed husbands of his sisters farming with his father now.

"You know, don't you, about Chris's 1930s vegetable truck sitting in the garage? He dreams about getting it going again."

"A 1930s vegetable truck?"

"Yes, but before you get too excited, you should also know that you are being fattened for the role of son-in-law."

"Whose?" he said.

"Not sure," I said. "Aunt Gracia and Fimi are fighting it out. Varti says Aunt Gracia has first dibs. Personally, I think I would be a bad choice. Varti was right. You're too young and sweet for both of us."

"Shucks," he said. "So I can't have either of you. Just my luck. Friends then, aye?"

We shook on it.

By now Sean was sharing a lot of suppers with us: Fimi had the advantage over his boarding house — she had produce to use up, so there might be several weeks' worth of stuffed tomatoes to take care of, or vats of carrot soup, enough for Varti's Armenians and all of us and Sean besides. He must be lonely in the evenings, after all, a country boy with no family in town.

"Maybe," Varti said, "that television wasn't such a good idea."

"Don't be so selfish," Fimi said.

Sean was starting to make the popcorn. Sammi was falling asleep in his lap. Aunt Gracia was mildly triumphant.

I sewed on hooks and eyes, thousands and thousands of hooks and eyes onto chaste white brassieres, riding the trail of white thread to wander snowy fields and valleys. I wasn't alone. Ara popped through the metal eyes behind me. Sammi was there. I asked to be moved to a machine. The needle would pound down on the fabric; Ara and Sammi would stay out of the way. But the clatter of the machines created an enormous silence, the silence of the waves on the shore, of the wind across the plains. The needle tucked seeds into spring soil. I knelt on the sun-warmed earth, and Sammi played beside me.

None of the women would speak to me. The Italian women thought I was Italian and was refusing to speak Italian; the Greek women thought I was Greek and was refusing to speak Greek; the Jewish women thought I was Jewish and was refusing to speak Yiddish; the French Canadian women said my French was the wrong French, not French-Canadian French.

Sammi was drawing pictures with only the black and purple crayons. She didn't cry when I left in the morning. She looked confused, and when I came back at night, she held her arms out to me, silent and exhausted, reaching for me as if she wasn't sure it was me. As Mama had reached for me.

# CHAPTER 15

I quit. I had managed six months, just long enough to miss the summer and the fall leaves, and just in time for the long, long winter nights.

"If you hated it so much," Varti said, "what were you trying to prove?"

"To prove I could, I guess," I said. "To forget. To be too busy to drink. Remember?"

"Oh. Right. Well, it worked, we have to admit that. But I guess it wasn't the job you were meant to have."

"Yup," I said. "And nope." We were all learning to talk like her, Sammi practising various garbled forms of, "Oh, my god, I forgot to take out the bloody garbage!" and "Not that record again!" Varti was cleaning up her language.

The records had been additional ammunition to keep me home sober and happy. Evening passes were restricted and required an accompanying guard. I missed the jazz rhythms and the stretched-out notes of the clarinet. I missed the ripples of light on the pool of my martini. Fortunately, Oscar Peterson was back in town, one of our Montreal boys, proof that warm piano could come from the cold north. Varti had a crush on Oscar's hands, those tinkly, nimble, playing hands. Sean was coming with us.

I had been restricted to one drink. I liked to savour the journey into oblivion, a slow drift into a glow of bass cello and mellow hands. You need more than one drink for that. I ordered tonic water and lemon, the poor man's gin and tonic, just to prove I could.

I missed my hangovers. At least they let me know I was alive.

Snow was piling up in the park. Sammi and I went out and left footprints. In the winter dawn, they were set in amethyst and gold.

Christmas was coming. Santa Claus. Christmas trees. Candy canes. Walking in a winter wonderland. Last year we had played it down. Now a Christmas tree was leaning against the railing on the front landing. Sean had brought it. He had promised Sammi a tree. Varti had a mild panic attack. Up to now, Aunt Gracia was all wide-eyed enthusiasm, but she couldn't keep it up. She would short-circuit. Varti didn't want to tip the balance with a Christmas tree. "Don't be silly, Varti," Aunt Gracia said. "Trees were symbols of life long before you Christians came along. Does that mean no one else can have it just because you people want it?"

"See what I mean?" Varti said. "She's way too rational."

Aunt Gracia was no longer afraid to go out. She had been talked into buying a fur coat by the furrier around the corner — a black seal coat that would bring out the fire in her black eyes and the silver in her hair. And why not, with leftover bits of this and that, make a matching coat for her button-sized granddaughter?

They looked like little black bugs.

I borrowed Aunt Gracia's coat and sneaked out for a Christmas drink, although really I had thought that I was simply taking Sammi for a walk to show her the fat, fluffy snowflakes falling out of the twilight, feathering beds for angels. Mama had said that snow was the kindest way to die, the kindest, surest escape. Before I knew it, though, we had crossed the park and were standing inside the doorway of a new nightclub. It was early. We were the only ones there. The bartender admired our matching coats and made us beef sandwiches. We had healthy drinks, hot milk for Sammi, hot milk and Kahlua for me. Varti found us.

"Just in time," I said. "I promised Luke — this is Luke — that I would take Sammi home before the drunks or his boss arrived."

"Well, at least we never have to worry about you being too stupid to come in from the cold."

"But I'm not drunk," I said. "Okay, maybe I'm a teeny bit drunk. Never drink hot milk and Kahlua on an empty stomach. Not enough milk. That's the problem. Oh, I forgot. It wasn't empty. I had a beef sandwich. Funny. All that bread should have soaked up the Kahlua. Are you going to yell at me?"

"Heavens, no," Varti said. "I've got myself to blame. I was the one who introduced you to this, although, stupid me, I didn't expect you to take to it with such flying colours. I should have known better. You take to everything with flying colours. Maybe I'll just cry instead."

"Don't. You never cry. I'll be good. How about if I only get drunk once a month? Not too drunk. Just, let's say, tipsy."

"I think I would be making a bargain with the devil."

It was Christmas Eve. Sammi and I had made gingerbread star cookies; Sammi had drawn Christmas cards for everyone in happy colours; Sean's mother sent straw decorations, pigs and ducks and miniscule bundles of dried tobacco tied with tiny perky red bows. The tree was up and decorated, and we had walked to midnight mass over crunchy snow. Aunt Gracia came along. Sammi was her granddaughter, too, and she was finished with battles. Who was to say one religion was better than another? Children took on the beliefs they were born into. Maybe there was something to candles and incense and gracious spaces, something to the hope in a tree of life and the reality of Christ's suffering. Life wasn't easy; no point in pretending it was.

I didn't want Sammi growing up with a message of suffering. It wasn't the message I wanted. I took out Ara's maps. We had been Armenian long before we had become Christian. Uncle Samuel had said, in the middle of the Father Havonissian/Aunt Gracia/Aisha Hanim battles, that one man's religion was another man's superstition; I was in the enviable position of being able to search out the truths in common in at least three of man's great religions.

"I don't want her growing up thinking that her religion is better than anyone else's," I said. "We didn't come here for that."

"Then Christmas is a good place to start," Varti said. "It's a peaceful story — and it's got a tree. I'm all for worshipping trees and geese."

"You're both heathens," Sean said. Sean was not.

We were going with Sean and Sammi to the rink in the park in front of his boarding house to try their new skates. He had never had a chance to really learn to skate: there had been only a river near the farm to learn to skate on, and by the time the snow had been cleared off lumpy ice, they had all wanted to give up and go home for hot chocolate. He wasn't sure that the hot chocolate hadn't been the drawing card right from the beginning.

Varti and I were watching from the sidelines, snug as bugs in rugs in our mothers' fur coats. Red cardinals were flashes of colour in the bare trees. Black-capped chickadees chicka-dee-dee-dee'd.

Varti was only interested in the view that was Sean.

"You know, kid," Varti said. "I can't keep my hands off that delicious farmer boy's body, and he won't sleep with me because I'll think he's taking advantage of me. It's making me distracted. If he doesn't take me to bed soon, I'm going to drive into a lamppost. I've got my tombstone all picked out ready to be engraved: 'Spurned Widow Dies of Lack of Sex.'"

"What?" I said. "When did this happen?"

"While we were keeping you sober. And maybe while he was fixing my car. You'd be amazed at what that boy can do with one hand."

"Oh," I said. "I see. Well, maybe you should pretend you're not interested. Remind him that you just want to be friends. That will depress him. In the meantime, remember that you can always ask one of the guys to pinch-hit. I have to say, though, I think most of them are lousy lovers. They wouldn't even notice if you weren't there."

"Nobody was forcing you."

"Yup," I said. "You're right. Never let it be said sex was forced on Sosi."

"You could have spoken up for yourself, pipsqueak."

"Oh, no, not me. Never let it be said that this half-breed slut speaks up for herself."

"Sometimes I want to slap you. You aren't a slut — you were never a slut. You were a kid who got carried away with her boyfriend. How long are you going to feel sorry for yourself? You win some, you lose some. Maybe Ara will come back, maybe he won't. So what?"

"So what?"

"Yeah. So what? Get on with it. You owe it to — life. I keep telling you, grab it while you can. Which doesn't mean getting sloshed and sleeping with every Tom, Dick, and Harry. You act as though you have no control over your life."

"I don't," I said. "I never have."

"Don't be ridiculous. If we go back far enough, none of us have. Maybe if you were still in your village in the mountains, you wouldn't have. God knows that there are plenty of places where women don't have choices. But you do. You keep trying to conveniently forget that you have a daughter, and that you're here, and it wasn't because of magic carpets. I mean, don't get me wrong, you've got things to feel sorry for yourself about, but enough's enough. For heaven's sake, pull up your socks. Count your blessings."

Sean and Sammi were back. They were both covered in snow. I dusted snow off Sammi, and Varti dusted the snow off Sean. "How about, Sean, sweetie," she said, "some hot wine instead of hot chocolate? We're grown-ups now."

"Okey-doke," he said.

I pulled up my socks. I started photographing my blessings. It was an entirely new way to think. Blessings had a wide definition, a steaming cup of coffee on the windowsill, sparrows chirping on the balcony railing for Sammi's morning rations.

Sean still wasn't sleeping with Varti. He had offered to open a garage with her instead. It would be swell: a dame who looked like dynamite in overalls and grease and a natural fixing kind of guy.

"So," Varti reported, "I said, 'Yeah, right. We should do a booming business. At least one of the two other cars on this street belongs to the local hoodlum with his own car fixing connection for those bullet-proof door panels. The other one gets tinkered with almost every Sunday by its proud owner and his two sons. Besides, you're a guy with only one arm. How are you going to do that?' And do you know what he said? 'Like I do everything else. With grace.' What am I going to do with him?"

He hadn't blushed around her for weeks. He radiated fondness. It made her nervous. It made her blush. There was only one tactic left, she said. Marriage.

It made me nervous.

She would be leaving.

Sammi would grow up and get married.

Aunt Gracia and Fimi and Chris would die, and I would be left alone.

"Wow!" Varti said. "Life goes quicker than I thought. Can't turn your back on it for a second. Wait ten minutes. You'll be a grandmother. You have to slow life down."

"Gin's slow."

"Too slow. Don't joke." She tore the pie dough she was rolling out. Sean liked pies. For the first time in her life, Varti was trying to cook. I snapped her picture, another one of my blessings. Or proof that she had actually taken up domestic pleasures.

"You're obsessed," Varti said. "Have you noticed? You are obsessed with reducing life to small squares."

"I am?"

"You are."

"So?"

"So there are other possibilities. Sean and I have been talking. We've found the perfect solution. It's been staring us in the face all the time. I don't know why none of us thought of it before. Photography. A studio. It isn't as if you don't have the experience. You worked with Meri. You know all the tricks of the trade."

"Gee," I said. "What do I think?"

"You think it's a great idea. What have you got to lose? You're in a rut, and your obsession with pictures is costing us a fortune."

"Where do you and Sean plan that I do the developing? In the bathroom? In your future garage?"

"There have been developments. While you were miserable in the factory or getting blotto, things have been happening. Momsy and Dadsy are getting out of the vegetable business. No more haggling over rotten lemons. From now on, he'll have leisurely breakfasts with Ma and Aunt Gracia. Ma can hardly wait. Leisurely breakfasts are her idea of romance. I'm not sure Pops is prepared."

"So am I taking over the vegetables?"

"No. No more vegetables. Zaven is sending carpets. Pops is going into the carpet business. We're going to put in a darkroom at the back. You might as well get set up to do your own developing, and the beauty of it is, you can, in the comfort and safety of Dad's shop surrounded by all your loved ones. You should know something about that. Weren't you always hanging around Zaven's and Uncle Samuel's shops when you were a kid? Sammi can go with you. Aunt Gracia can stop in for tea. Ma will stop by and measure you guys for outfits. It'll be perfect."

Even Aunt Gracia thought it was a great idea. Her distrust of the camera, under serious assault at Meri's, had completely evaporated: she had never been superstitious — where had I gotten that idea? Now she was sorry she didn't have pictures of me when I was small. You forget, she said.

"Then you will be happy to know," I said, "that Mariam's mother took pictures behind your back for years."

She was happy to know. I handed over the stack of photos Aimée had sent before we left Jerusalem, along with some of Meri's, and Aunt Gracia pasted her past all over her bedroom walls: Maurice and Aimée unrecognizably youthful in front of the Eiffel Tower; Aunt Gracia asleep on the beach under her hat; Mariam, a dutiful schoolgirl in her school uniform, and me, not. I was everywhere, a bewildered seven-year-old, a defiant ten, a hopeful fourteen, a surprised and pregnant sixteen. Mariam, in contrast, at no matter what age, was eternally gentle and sweet. It was a miracle, Aunt Gracia said, that Mariam's mother had never managed to get Mariam on a day when I'd been torturing her.

It was spring. Snow shrank before our eyes. The sidewalks were clear. A redheaded woodpecker thumped celebration on the tree in front of the house. The vegetables and shelves had been banished, and Ami's carpets had arrived. Sammi could lounge around on piles of carpets, the embodiment of "The Princess and The Pea." My new professional camera stood confidently on its tripod, and the darkroom was cozy and warm.

Eventually Varti noticed that the photographs my studio produced weren't commercial. The fruit seller didn't want a picture of himself napping behind crates of Macintosh apples. The downstairs neighbour ranted for days after I snapped her bending over a wicker basket of diapers. The money was in studio work, the identical smile, the identical brush cut and beauty shop perm. No one, Varti said, wanted a bad day at the fruit stand for posterity. Karsh (fellow Armenian, let that be a lesson to me) had the right idea. Make people beautiful, interesting, striking. Leave their problems at home.

I practised on the Armenian families, Dad behind, Mom demure on a chair, the children starched and shining, all future and no past; I practised on the shop owners up and down the street, the waitress and the hairdresser, the poultry seller and the baker and the tool-die maker. In their suits and best dresses, you couldn't tell who had spent the day with bobby pins in her teeth or who had spent the day covered in feathers. All were contented women and men. They wanted copies for the shop, for their mother in Italy, for the cousin in Winnipeg.

I started making money and enjoying it, the first time since delivering coffee and feeding worms.

Aunt Gracia sat for a photograph with Sammi. She had her teeth in and her bifocals off and a tiny white bun at the back of her head. She was so adorable I almost cried. Sammi laughed. Sammi thought cameras were a joke.

Aunt Gracia sent photos of herself to Mariam's mother, to Ara's parents, to Meri. Especially to Meri. Meri had been inundating us with snapshots since she had moved to Lebanon: Meri with a stack of story apples, Meri on a beach with her own plastic pail, Meri under a pile of young grandsons. She was also posting regular holiday bulletins. We may have been safely in a Christian country able to manage Christmas and Easter (possibly Lent), but there were other holy days: *Anarageen*, the third Sunday of Lent when the prodigal son returned; *Poon Parengentan*, the last Sunday before Lent when the first parents, Adam and Eve, were celebrated. *Poon Parengentan* had been Mama's only clear memory of a holy day, for on these days the whole village was topsy-turvy: her father was the priest, the priest was the shopkeeper, the shopkeeper was the teacher, the teacher was the tax collector... There were engagements, and weddings, and feasts. The engagements and weddings still happened, but there was no theatre in the streets.

Fimi was infuriated: "So that's the kind of friend she is. One of those old country Armenians, high-hatting us as if we have no idea who we are or where we have come from."

"Uh-oh," Varti said. "Now we're in for it. A new apple war. The last one with I don't remember who, some do-gooder relative who lived to regret the day, started when I was a kid and was still going on when I left the country. Wait. It will spread. Ma's got more troops now."

We were all enlisted. Supplying information was easy, or at least it would have been if it hadn't resulted in arguments about recipes and whether the *Catholicos* in Armenia (Soviet Armenia) was really our *Catholicos* or just a Soviet stooge and whether we should sully ourselves by taking on a Christmas that wasn't Orthodox and whether Armenians who weren't religious were truly Armenian after all. Fimi started telling stories that Varti had only dim memories of, and Varti was expected to write them out so Fimi could send them to Meri for the grandsons: no doubt Meri was too busy worrying about ruining her skin with too much sun (after all, she wore a different fashionable hat in each picture) to be telling stories. If she even remembered them in the first place.

All Fimi's stories had a moral, her favourite, told particularly if Varti happened to be home, was Don't Judge a Bear by His Clothing, which even Sammi recognized as an encoded don't-pass-over-a-prince-disguised-as-a-mere-mailman ("Is Sean a hungry bear?"): you never know when that pesky bear cub who was driving the king to distraction with his enormous appetite would turn out to be an enchanted prince with as much appetite for doing good as he had had for food. Fimi had no idea that the relationship had changed.

Stories weren't good for Sammi. I was never sure who she was, or who I was supposed to be. Sometimes I was a hungry fisherman who hadn't had a good dinner in over a week, but I was so kind-hearted that when I pulled up a talking fish (Sammi), I allowed myself to be talked into throwing the fish back into the water (the park). I would be rewarded, though, because no good deed is wasted. God sees it. Like the fisherman, I would find myself at the losing end of a bad bargain with the devil, and she, that yappy fish, would save me.

At the end of each of Fimi's stories, there were three apples for Sammi to share out, one for the teller of the tale, one for the listeners, and one for whomever they wished to share the story with, for stories were meant to be shared.

Mama, at the end of one of her stories, had always given me three of something, anything: three bits of coloured wool, three brightly coloured pebbles. There were never any apples. We were too high in the mountains for apples. I had known apples no better than I had known Jesus.

The trees were budding. The grass in the park was green. We were putting pots of flowers out, getting ready to plant herbs in window boxes.

Varti and Sean were getting married. I bought a bottle of gin. Varti smashed it on the sidewalk. Then she ordered me to get a broom and dustpan to sweep it up: "Listen, pipsqueak. You're not holding me hostage with your alcohol. If you don't shape up, I'll send Aunt Gracia and Sammi back to Mariam. Mariam will win. Is that what you want?"

"I'm young and inexperienced."

"You're irresponsible," she said. "That's different. Do you want your kid to be an orphan? Do you think Aunt Gracia is kidding? How do you think Sammi is going to feel if Aunt Gracia suddenly defects back to Mariam with her? Does the word 'abandoned' mean anything to you?"

"You could always keep Sammi. That wouldn't be so bad."

"You wish. Do you think Aunt Gracia would go without her if she thought you were on the skids?"

"Easy come, easy go," I said. "Now you see 'em, now you don't. Mariam won a long time ago, you know. Maybe before I was born."

She slapped me.

"Go ahead. Spoil your life with all your 'poor me' if you want to." She left me outside on the steps under the patterns of the moon.

It had been a long time since I had looked up at the moon. I'd left the moon behind. Ara had stolen the moon.

Varti was paying a lot of attention to Sammi. In preparation, she said, for me turning into a slut and ending up on the streets.

"She'll be an orphan," I said.

"No kidding," she said.

"I don't want her to be an orphan."

"Tell it to someone else."


When Varti and Sean were married, I was the photographer. She wore Uncle Samuel's poppy red blouse with gold slacks so that Sean would never forget how valuable she was or why she was marrying him. For his body. There was only the ritual glass of wine shared by the bride and groom and godparents, even though I swore by Christ on the cross (she was getting married in a Catholic church by a Catholic priest) that I never drank on the job. The bride and groom were joined by a golden chain, a gift from his parents. They hadn't come. It was too cold, Montreal was too far, who would feed the pigs and chickens? It almost stopped the wedding. "They don't like me," Varti said. "I'm not good enough for them. I'm not a Catholic farm girl. I've done it again. First a nice Jewish boy whose parents are ready to jump off cliffs at the thought of an Armenian daughter-in-law, then a black guy who rejects me — now an Irish Catholic."

"I thought I was Armenian," Sean said. "What happened to that?"

"Ask your mother," Varti said.

Fimi wrote to his mother. The truth was, she wrote back, Nick wasn't ready for so many Armenians, not after so many years.

My photographs were a hit. I became a wedding regular, a christening specialist, particularly good with exhausted brides and worried babies. I got a reprieve. I could go to the clubs as long as I didn't drink. I'd proved, after all, that I could order tonic and lemon. Varti had a secret weapon: a letter from Mariam confirming that she would be happy to have any or all of us any time: "Your choice," Varti said. "Not much you can do about it if you're drunk."

I carried the letter with me tucked into my dainty nightclub bag. Silk. Beaded. A gift from Uncle Samuel to Aunt Gracia in their younger days. It wouldn't hurt, Aunt Gracia said, to have Uncle Samuel with me: I would never have behaved this way if he were alive. I wouldn't have wanted to hurt him.

I was dreaming about Ara.

On *Anarageen*, the third Sunday of Lent, when we were supposed to be commemorating the return of the Prodigal

Son (Meri's reminder), a telegram arrived from Nissim. "Misplaced shipment located. New shipping fees. Renegotiating." There was no indication of the condition of the merchandise. It could be unrecognizable.

"Oh, my god," Varti said. "Can you believe it? Who would have believed it? He's alive. I can't believe it. Would you believe it? Thank god. Now he can come and look after you."

Everybody wanted him to come, even Aunt Gracia, who at one time told me to stab her and get it over with whenever his name came up. I was the only exception, although Sammi seemed to be on my side. She was old enough to have opinions beyond "I don't want to go to bed yet." Now when Aunt Gracia show her pictures of *Baba* and said he was coming, Sammi announced, "I don't know him. Sean is my dad."

"See?" I said. "Who says we want him to come? Besides, what he'll really want is for us to go there, and we're not."

A letter came from Ara's father. Ara had been caught for "fomenting revolution." Looking for "secret" Armenians to help "escape" was clearly "subversive," Turkey being, after all, a free and democratic country where all religions were treated equally. It seemed that his parents had no intention of keeping him in Jaffa. They would meet him in Beirut, and send him to Montreal. He needed to be away so he could forget what he had been through, and, not least, so he would never be tempted to go back.

Chris and Fimi trumpeted Ara's heroism to the entire community.

"Varti," I said. "Can't I get drunk just once? Isn't a wounded tortured husband you haven't seen in over three years an excuse? Maybe if I get drunk enough, I'll remember who he is and why I liked him. Because I really really really don't like him. Do I have to like a husband who deserted me just so he could be thrown in jail? Why did I like him, Varti?"

"His hands," Varti said. "You said something about his hands. And then you got pregnant. I don't know why you liked him. Women are stupid. Why did you like him?"

"You told me to."

"Did I? O god — I did. Well, I was wrong. I made a mistake. The signs were there, too, right from the beginning, fighting over Soviet Armenia at the art gallery, baiting the guards at the gates. How could I have been so stupid? Still, lots of arguers argue without risking their necks in Turkey. How was I to know?"

I went AWOL. I sneaked off when everyone was off duty, and found my drummer, and got gloriously drunk. I slept it off on a pile of Ami Zaven's rugs, and even had a photo to show for it. Drum and single martini. The martini balanced delicately on the rim of the drum. A one-shot wonder.

On Holy Monday when the house was filled with flowers in celebration of the creation of the universe, another telegram was delivered. "Shipment undamaged. Value unchanged."

"Ha!" Aunt Gracia said. "What did I tell you?"

The dreams changed. Sammi was looking for Ara in a field of sunflowers with their backs to the sun.

A third telegram arrived: "Shipment confirmed delivered Beirut."

And a fourth: "Shipment en route to Montreal."

"Talk about a man of few words," Varti said. She was slathering butter and honey on a fat chunk of *choereg*, sweet bread. Lent was over: butter and honey were back. A sweet year was assured. "Poor you," Varti said. "No wonder you're nervous. Sammi won't even remember him. I mean, you've been separated longer than you were together. What if he's changed? What if you hate him? Lots of marriages broke down after the war, and the soldiers coming back were fighting for a good cause. Ara was fighting for a lost cause. No wonder you're mad at him. I'd be ready to shoot him. Or maybe myself."

"Do you have a gun?" I said.

"Sorry," she said. "Sometimes my mouth talks before I know what it is going to say. Mom said she never had to worry what I was up to when I was a kid because I told her everything. 'Guess what we did at recess, Mom? We smoked in the bathroom.' At least you won't have to worry about Ara getting into trouble here. He won't find a Turk for love or money. Out of sight, out of mind. And what's taking that shipment so long to arrive? He should have been here weeks ago."

"Maybe he's got things to do. Like liberate all the Armenians from Turkey."

"You sound bitter. You're too young to be bitter."

"I'm not too young for anything."

# CHAPTER 16

Ara walked down the steps from the airplane in a halo of September light, placing each foot with deliberation as though it were the last thing he was going to do. He almost walked right into us.

"That's *Baba*," I said to Sammi.

She moved behind me out of eye range. She was thigh height now, still with popping curls, ever-startling blue eyes, and Ara's full delicious mouth.

"She's afraid of me," he said.

"What did you expect?" I said.

Fortunately, Varti had decided that after being cooped up for months with a bunch of men and then popped across the ocean, Ara would need to be "oriented."

"— Uum," Varti said. "What do you say we take the scenic route home?"

He took out a cigarette. It had been cut in half. He lit it. He didn't offer me the other half.

"Didn't you want me to come back?" he asked.

"It depends on when you're leaving again. There's always another Armenian to rescue."

"Not by me," he said. "I'm not very good at it."

Sammi sat between us, huddling against me, away from Ara, watching.

It wasn't what I had intended to say. I had been telling Sammi, "*Baba* is going to sing to you." I had tried to rehearse, even though I was terrified: "Welcome home. This is your beautiful daughter. How've you been?" "Hello, darling, long time no see." "Hello. Let me introduce myself, Sosi Mamoulian, mother of your child. Perhaps you don't remember me." "Hi there, big boy. What's a guy like you doing in a place like this?"

I had asked Sean what guys want when they came home from the war: "A bath," Sean said. "Dry blankets. A night with the girl. Mom. The cat. A beer with Dad. You never know. It'll be okay."

I could feel that it wasn't going to be okay.

I ached to be held.

I ached for a dreamless sleep.

As long as Varti kept talking, I was safe, and Varti could talk a long time: first, Ara would notice that this was a land of dark perfumed forests, wet and spongy underfoot with birds, bats, and bugs hiding in the foliage. There were, she had heard, sand dunes on the upper shore of the St. Lawrence, but even so it was a different kind of desert, half the year under snow, nothing like the desert where man had learned to live like a lizard under a rock, swaddling himself in yards of black cloth (why black?) to keep perspiration from escaping so he wouldn't dry up and blow away.

Before her life on blooming deserts, Varti's idea of nature had been to stick her head out of the door to see whether she needed overshoes to get to work. She couldn't have differentiated between an oak and chestnut to save her soul. Now she marveled at anything that grew without benefit of a watering pail or a hoe, and she knew them all, right down to sugar maple, black maple, silver maple, red maple, Norway maple. Our cathedrals should be the forests. That's where God lived. On the desert, you were never sure whether you were in the presence of God or whether He had gone for lunch. Wasn't home.

We were coming back to industry, the ports and exploited dockworkers. Montreal was a thriving metropolis with the flavour of France and the business acumen of America, the financial centre of the country because of a geographical accident — the ships stopped here. From here on, it was shallows and rapids. Anything and anyone going west has to be shifted onto the rails, through forests, across prairie, over mountains, and down to the sea. Sea to shining sea.

Now we were going up to the lookout on Mount Royal to give him a lay of the land. Green copper roofs lay below; Victoria Hospital, all limestone turrets and towers; greystone and red brick row housing; and a gleaming band of blue bordering the island. Beyond was the south shore, flat planes with a single low blue mountain in the distance.

Varti had run down. Sammi was sneaking closer to Ara. She was letting him play games with her hands. We were going home.

"What's wrong with you?" Varti said to me as we were walking up the steps. "You could be a bit friendly. It wouldn't kill you. The poor guy's just escaped from prison. You were probably the only thing that kept him going."

"I don't like him," I said. "Who is he?"

She panicked.

"Of course you do. You're married to him. Look what he's been through. Oh, Lord. Look. You're just nervous. Relax. He's still gorgeous. But in a different way. No wonder you fell for him."

"Is that the reason I fell for him? How shallow! Well, it's good that one of us remembers. Too bad it isn't me."

"At least you can still laugh."

"Who's laughing?"

I didn't know what to say to him: how was prison? what did you do all day? did you make any friends? how did Nissim find you? how much did it cost to get you out? how did you get enough food to survive? how did you survive?

Ara was the last one up the stairs. Sean was waiting for him at the top. He put an arm around his shoulder: "How you doing, bud?"

"Don't know," Ara said. "I have absolutely no idea."

Sean and Ara liked each other. There was an instant been-through-the-war sympathy. Sammi fell asleep on Ara's lap. Aunt Gracia took her to bed with her. I wanted her back. For protection. But Ara fell asleep without touching me. I cried. I hated myself for crying. I didn't come from criers. And what was I crying about? Because the man I didn't like didn't like me?

I woke up in the middle of the night missing Sammi's squirmy little body. Ara was up sitting at the dressing table in the dark patiently cutting cigarettes in half.

"You don't have to do that," I said. I took a cigarette. A whole, uncut cigarette. "I'm making money with bad photographs. We can afford cigarettes."

"Who taught you to smoke?"

"I'm a quick learner," I said. "I don't need anyone to teach me."

"You've changed," he said.

"No kidding," I said. "We're not photographs, you know. You don't put us up on the mantelpiece and expect us to be the same when you get back. We're even in full living colour."

He was holding his cigarette, unlit. In the old country, smoking was refined, the men gathering around the water pipe under the grape arbour. In the old country, women and children were respected and were respectable. The pipe was a ceremony.

I didn't dare smoke in my bedroom. Varti and Sean, now living in the apartment above us, didn't smoke in their own home. Aunt Gracia wouldn't let Sammi up to play if she knew they had been smoking, and she always knew.

According to Aunt Gracia, I was puffing all day, polluting my lungs, destroying the health of all those around me, burning up Uncle Samuel's hard-earned legacy, shaming my name, shaming Aunt Gracia, letting people think I'd grown up on the street, reminding her daily of the mistake she had made losing her heart to me, and now there wasn't just me, but Sammi as well. She used to think that I had a mind of my own, but suddenly I had become the perfect sheep, a butterfly flying into the sun, beating my wings against all sense and reason.

I had been thinking of taking up cigars. They were satisfying in the hand. A small box of cigars had arrived from my drummer. He was playing in Cuba, a hot country. I was welcome to join him. It would do me good, unfreeze my soul, do what neither he nor the gin had been able to do. He had a tan, he said. All over. I'd like him better.

Aunt Gracia had handed me the package accusingly.

She had been counting on Ara to save me.

I gave Ara an edited version, cutting the drummer and cigars: "Aunt Gracia expects you to save me."

"Poor Aunt Gracia," Ara said. He laughed. He laughed until he cried.

Sammi came padding in. Ara bundled her into bed with him and told her a story about a foolish king who allowed himself to be swallowed up by a dragon. Many tried to rescue him, strong men and mighty armies, yet it was the smile of his tiny princess daughter that set him free. She didn't believe any of it, but she fell asleep.

Then I remembered: I liked him when he told stories. I liked him when he loved Sammi. I didn't want to remember liking him.

He slept with Sammi in his arms. I went out to the front landing. It was a warm night, and the street was endless welcoming shadows. The leaves rustled.

The next day was spent on preparing a Middle-Eastern feast for Ara. It had been weeks in the planning. Fimi and Chris were used to making do, honey instead of pomegranate syrup, vanilla instead of rosewater, walnuts instead of pistachios. Now, because of the length and breadth of the hunt, a new electric refrigerator shared my darkroom, humming comfortingly. We ate on the back balcony in the September light with fat yellow chrysanthemums and red hollyhocks in flowerpots around us, our courtyard. The neighbours on the balconies across the way, all three floors, looked up, across, and down, congratulating me on the return of my husband. They were sure he was going to like it here.

Ara didn't eat. He was out of the habit, he said. He was drinking, though, arak and *labhan*. The arak loosened him up. He held up his glass of *labhan* to the fading evening light, and launched into a eulogy on *labhan,* the perfect food, all digestion, nourishing the sick, the old, the weak. (You can talk about *labhan* for hours without once stumbling on the word "prison.") He would have thought that, in a civilized country like Canada was supposed to be, there would be a street seller on every corner, a bronze urn balanced on a tray slung from his shoulders, a bronze ladle dangling enticement. But no. He had to remember that what was civilized to some was primitive to others. Barbaric.

He couldn't have hit on a subject closer to Aunt Gracia's heart: Aunt Gracia had nurtured a jar of yoghurt across the Atlantic as if, by ensuring the safe arrival of that glass jar, she was ensuring the three of us. Diasporas were the coming thing. Wandering grandmothers were the sign of the times. The past had to be acknowledged, incorporated, otherwise it ate you up. Yoghurt was the first thing Aunt Gracia checked in the morning, and the last at night, making sure it was warm, out of drafts, doling it out like ancient knowledge.

"Ancient knowledge," Ara said. Turkey was ancient knowledge, the story of the ages carved by both wind and man, with nature's hand the most enduring. Man, our courtyards and our vineyards, our monuments and our graves, melted into the land, into the wind. Into time. Perhaps we ought to be better at accepting our melting quality. At giving up.

"'Turkey?'" I said finally. "What happened to 'Asia Minor'?"

"'Turkey' is a new word," he said. "I use it as often as I can so I won't forget it."

I hardly saw Ara after that — he kept himself surrounded by friendly troops. The Armenians adopted him. He was a hero. Daniel emerging out of the lions' den.

With the Armenians, he tried to pretend that life was normal, that Armenians were living a free, normal life, no longer victims, out of the crossfire. That was all we wanted, to live a free normal life. But there was always some crisis, a doctor bill, papers denied, rent, streetcar fare, ink, shoelaces. Always there was desperation to bring over a father, a mother, a younger brother before there was more slaughter.

"What's normal?" Varti said, breaking into one of her Freda-like fits of hysterical laughter.

Ara was learning to fix engines. He liked the silence of machines and good work done at the end of the day. He liked Sean, the farmer who believed that there would be another season. Sean introduced Ara to taverns. Every second Saturday night (all that Varti would allow), they came home drunk, told prison/army jokes: "Come again when you don't have to stay so long"; "How did you find your steak?" "Oh. I thought it was a turd. I fed it to the prison rat." They sat together on the carpet and had long meaningful discussions on man's inhumanity to man. Ara believed in good tribes and bad, the good nurtured on Christ and talking fish and kindly bears, and the bad on cruel sultans.

"Nah," Sean said. "We're all the same, bud," and he would deliver incontrovertible proof: the allied commanders, good white Christians every one, had committed atrocities against their own soldiers. Boys who were shell-shocked and completely mad, who had fever and could barely stand, were sent back into battle over and over again. They were sent back until they didn't come back. He was lucky. He had finally lost an arm — before he went crazy and while he could still walk. You could crack almost anybody if you left him hungry, wet, and cold for days on end. With no end in sight. You could make them believe almost anything. Lose faith in almost anything. He wouldn't have believed it if he hadn't seen it himself, guys beside him lying in shit and blood and begging him to end the pain.

Anyone who grew up on a farm knew about the kindness of ending the pain.

"You see, bud," Sean said. "We're all the same. You got your good guys and your bad, and sometimes the good guys aren't so good and the bad guys aren't so bad. You can't just sit back and decide you know who's who and what's what. The story's never over. You never know, one day the flying carpet might be offering free rides to talking fish."

"Shshshsh," Ara would say, "not in front of the women and children."

And they would fall asleep on the carpet in each other's arms, last bastion against man's inhumanity to man.

At the end of three months, Ara was rebuilding engines.

I needed a drink. Ara was having all the fun. I wanted a night out on the town.

Varti panicked: "If you want to break up your marriage, just introduce him to your bed partners. Is that what you want?"

"What marriage?" I said.

"Don't be so shallow," she said. "There's more to marriage than just sex."

"Really?" I said.

While Ara and I had been carefully not touching each other, Varti and Sean were enthusiastically, ecstatically, splendidly pregnant. They giggled and flirted and teased. I was jealous. I wanted another child wrapped around my leg. I wanted her happy pregnancy.

We all went out for a night on the town. There was safety in numbers, and Varti was riding shotgun. My former bed partners were respectful: "Hey, man. Welcome home. Your woman talked about you all the time. Wouldn't give any of us a chance." They were lying. They hadn't heard about him at all, certainly not from me. Occasionally Varti told people only what they needed to know: "Use condoms, you bastard; if there are any diseases, I'll have your kneecaps rearranged. She's just wacko enough to get pregnant, too, and I've got enough problems."

They figured it was safer to believe her. She had enough friends to get their kneecaps rearranged for cheap.

I appreciated her concern. There was no room in my delicate little purse for a diaphragm. Nice girls didn't plan these things. It was bad for their reputations. I carried only cigarettes, a lighter, Mariam's letter, Sammi's picture, and money for one clear mountain gin.

Besides, since my drummer had left, I had fallen victim to involuntary chastity. It was a loyalty thing. The guys were protecting me for him from each other.

Ara was a surprise. They had thought I was a widow.

When we got home at dawn, Ara sat on the edge of the bed, toying with an unlit cigarette.

"Do you think you'll ever want to make love to me again?" he said.

"I always want to make love to you. Morning, noon, and night, remember? What gave you the idea that I didn't?"

He took my hand. He stroked my fingers, one by one.

"I guess you weren't exactly suffering," he said.

"Who gets to decide the rules of suffering?" I said. He didn't take his hand away. But he stopped playing with my fingers. "Are you going to be an outraged husband? Threaten to have me stoned? Beaten to death? Circumcised? Tied out with the sheep and the goats?"

"I didn't come home a virgin. There's no reason why you should. Of course, I had an excuse. I was raped. The things you like about me, they liked. My lovely ass, my delicious mouth. But at least you don't have to worry about me expecting you to die to save my honour — sex isn't an honour worth dying for. We learn that in jail."

The prisoners who had it best were the ones who were appropriated by someone the others feared, or by someone who actually grew to love his lover. Then it might even be gentle. Then you might have a chance to heal.

"Heal?" I said.

Yes, he said. What did I think he had been doing in Lebanon for the past five months? When he first went in, he convinced himself that as long as he held us in his imagination, he would get out alive: "But then you disappeared, and there wasn't any reason I could remember to stay alive, so I fought back, and instead of being just raped, I got beaten up and then raped. By the time Nissim found me, I didn't have any fight left. I cried in his arms like a baby."

He hated himself — for wanting to come back to us so badly that he put up with anything to live, for not having the guts to die fighting. He hated himself for letting them win.

"They didn't," I said. "You survived."

He said I was naive. He no longer knew what he was capable of, either good or bad, and the fear I had described in my mother, the fear that overtakes all other emotions, all reason and thought, he now understood. If there was one thing that he would never forgive them for it was that he had been forced to learn things about himself that no man should have to learn.

"And you, my ever surprising wife? How about you?"

"That's me, surprising. I hear myself saying things I didn't know I thought, and the things I think I'm thinking don't seem to get to the front. I hardly ever hear myself say anything nice to anyone. Even to Aunt Gracia. I'm terrified of losing her. And I can't tell her. Something's wrong with me."

"Do you love me?"

"Of course."

"Say it. It would be nice to hear."

"You first."

He laughed. "You never were very good at it." He pulled me to him, and kissed the tip of my nose, and my body forgot what my mind was thinking. "We need practice."

I fell asleep wrapped around him.

Ara dreamed of the pictures he had taken. The photographs had been only a cover, an excuse, but the more he took, the more they mattered until, finally, it was all that mattered. He had photographed every bend in the Turkish Euphrates, every bank of dry grasses, every ravine, every well, stream, village, and field, and even as he had snapped the shutter, he knew that he had failed. The silence in the wind, the overgrown grasses, the tranquility of the waters was a lie. When they took his film, they had taken nothing.

# CHAPTER 17

"Hey, baby," Ara said. He was learning jazz English by leaps and bounds. "Why my Angel Eyes ain't here?" when I was late coming to bed, and "Pardon me, I got to run," when he left for work with Sean at the garage. He and Sammi sang together: they sang to me while I hung out clothes ("Nice Work If You Can Get It"); they sang when I agreed to go to the park ("Goody Goody"); they sang when I didn't ("Don't Be That Way"). Varti bought 45's, "Rock Around the Clock," "Diana," and "Little Darlin'," so we could keep up with the times.

Ara and Sammi sang all day, and I escaped to the darkroom. I liked him better than gin. It was frightening.

Ara was upset with the Armenians. Rumours were circulating that I had been less than the perfect mourning wife. Ara took the blame. He said he had abandoned me, left me alone in a strange land while he (stupidly: hadn't I warned him?) played hide and seek with the military. And then he stopped helping them build shelves or stack crates. "Hey, relax, bud," Sean said. "Human nature, remember? Your good guys and your bad." Varti was too busy to intervene. After the last one had his or her papers to stay in the country, she would worry about whether Armenians ought to be more perfect than other people and what you did with the ones who weren't. Right now it was enough that she was taking trains to Ottawa to beat down deportation orders, her baby beside her in a basket.

Varti had gone into labour while she was changing a carburetor in her and Sean's new garage. Sean offered to deliver the baby. He had delivered plenty of foals. He thought it must be pretty much the same.

"Next time," she said.

Sean had been expecting a tiny fighting Varti with too many opinions, not this entirely agreeable redheaded infant. He called his cuddly baby Tiger, his version of Ara's bid for Tigrane. He wasn't sure the kid was ready for the weight of the name of a two-thousand-year-old Armenian warrior king.

The leaves were starting to turn and fall and crunch garnet and gold under our feet.

"No wonder the country is so unpopulated," Aunt Gracia said. "There isn't enough time to grow a decent onion, let alone pomegranates." She had been released from courtyard walls only to be hemmed in by a fortress of impenetrable cold, as impenetrable as the long months, as impenetrable as death. The black sealskin coat hanging in the front hall closet no longer offered comfort.

But Sammi was excited. "There's a touch of fall in the air," she announced.

Ara said he could get used to it. Maybe my defection hadn't been such a bad idea. Maybe I'd done us all a favour. He was telling Sammi new stories about the Armenian tribes becoming a mighty nation, a nation without borders, a nation within nations. A new map tracing our Diaspora was in the making, along with a plot to bring a priest from the Old Quarter. We might even have our own schools. Our history might live.

I was getting used to doing wife things again, making Armenian coffee in the morning instead of perked coffee just because Ara liked it, massaging his neck after a hard day at the garage. The garage was doing a booming business. Chris had a new idea, to sell cars as well as fix them. His chattiness was surely destined for more than mere carpets. There was a future in mobility.

I told Ara everything, how much Aunt Gracia had worried, and how much I'd hated him — and how sometimes, floating on bubbles, I wasn't sure that his mother and my mother and I weren't all the same person.

And then I found a pistol in his drawer, tucked into a sock, nestled in letters, mad disjointed letters about "catching the wave of the horror of the Nazi camps," of "making the link between our genocide and the holocaust." It was the success of our genocide that had inspired Hitler: "Who remembers the Armenians?" Now was our chance to remind the world that Armenians remembered, that we had never been allowed to forget. Now was our chance to tell the world that there were still Armenians in Turkey who had to hide. He had been wrong to go in. It wasn't an "internal problem" at all. It was an external, international problem. We owed it to those inside to make it international.

I got drunk. I bought a bottle of gin and some wrinkled fall lemons and tonic water and maraschino cherries, fake red, fake sweet. They reminded me of hearts, tender hearts, tenderized hearts floating in gin. I sat on my mother's carpet with Ara's pistol. Pistols weren't all that bad. I was here, alive, because of a pistol. Or was it a sabre? My grandfather had killed once. He had taken Allah's name in vain, killed in the name of Allah. He had murdered an Armenian. Watched the light go out of someone's eyes. Mama was restitution, his gift of light.

Ara found me talking to his pistol, his letters scattered around me like fall leaves. I was telling the pistol how I almost liked Ara better than gin, like I almost liked the drummer better than gin. No one was as dependable as gin.

"Hey, babe," I said. "Look what I found."

He was angry. This was none of my business. Pistols had nothing to do with me.

"Whoa — hey! This is me, Angel Eyes, bearer of your seed, remember? You do know what people do with guns, don't you? They say it's not so much fun, watching the light go out of someone's eyes. Who are you planning to kill, anyway? Varti said I wouldn't have to worry about you: 'He won't find a Turk for love nor money. Out of sight, out of mind.'"

"There are Turks in every country. They're called diplomats. Ambassadors. War criminals."

"Oh, goody, that should be easy. Just walk up and shoot the Turkish Ambassador. Why didn't I think of that? Why don't you just shoot me? One Turk is as good as another. You might as well shoot Sammi, too, before she figures out that her father has a deep abiding hatred for all things Turk. Poor you, stuck with a Turkish daughter and a Turkish wife, and the only reason you have us at all is because of that Turkish god in the mountains. Then there are all the other nasty Turks, the one who taught me to add, the one who gave me my first job, Aisha Hanim, who I abandoned. Oh yes, and Mr. Monzour, too. Don't forget him. You know, the one who thinks we all have to learn to get along."

I left. I took the pistol with me. It belonged to me now. I took a cab to a bar. Any bar. Ara followed me. I left through a back door with a man, any man, who was surprised I didn't do it for money and who was glad when it was over because neither of us could do it at all. We sat on the bed and felt sorry for ourselves. I offered him the pistol. He thought I was being overly generous. Free non-sex was one thing, but free pistols another.

Ara was sitting on the front step in the smoke-tinted light of early dawn under a leafless tree smoking a whole uncut cigarette. He threw it away when he saw me coming.

I picked it up.

"Waste not, want not," I said. "You never know when you're going to need it."

He didn't want it.

"Oh, is your pride hurt? Are you going to rise up and smite me, or whatever it is you're supposed to do when your honour has been struck in the heart? It serves you right, lying about loving us more than life itself and then running off to be Jesus saving the world. Poor Jesus. You can't expect him to save you if you're so determined to destroy yourself. I'm putting the pistol back in your sock. If I thought you were worth it, I'd save you from yourself and throw it into the garbage, but I'm leaving it there so I'll never forget. It's my fault, anyway. Anyone can see that. Ask your mother. If it weren't for me, you wouldn't have left her and ended up in prison. I don't give a damn about your causes. I left to get away from tribes with causes. Oops, I forgot. You can't fight history. History repeats itself. I heard that somewhere. Mama — orphan. Sosi — orphan. Sammi. Orphan. Never fight history."

I staggered off to sleep on my mother's carpet. Ara followed me. "It's not as if I didn't know," I informed Mama in the carpet. "Never fall in love. Very dangerous. Very very dangerous."

Ara knelt at my side. He played with one of my curls. "I did it for you," he said, "my little moon-mad Sosi still up in the mountains with the stars in your hair. For all of you, for your grandfather forced off his mountain to commit murder, for you and your mother, expelled from Paradise and condemned to wander the earth."

"Don't do me any favours. I know what has condemned me. I know it better than you do. You're winning, though. Congratulations. The Armenian half — you know, Mama afraid to live — is winning. You can go off happy with the thought that Sammi has an alcoholic mother. Oh, I forgot. She'll be safe with Mariam. Perfect Mariam. You probably want that, anyway, so go away. Leave me alone."

He sent an emissary.

"You know, Sos, there are tribes with causes wherever you go," Sean said. "Even here."

"Not my causes, though," I said.

Ara brought a blanket and curled up on the floor beside me: "If the mountain won't come to Mohammed, then Mohammed must come to the mountain."

I bought a new bottle of gin and didn't drink it just to prove I could — not drink it, that is. But it would be there when I needed it, nestled on the letters beside the pistol sock. It disappeared one day, but I bought another one, just as beautiful, just as clear and sparkling.

A week later, we were still sleeping on the floor. Chris had contributed a carpet. A thick, new carpet, big enough for two, but I wasn't abandoning mine. I wasn't abandoning my mother.

Sometimes, when everyone was asleep, I got up and went back to the studio to work on a new series of uncommercial photographs, Still Life with Pistol. My favourite was with Sammi. Sleeping Child. I fell asleep on a field of carpets and wept for a lost unphotographable past.

Weeks passed, and nothing changed. My bottle was still there, nestled beside its pistol sock.

Ara followed me one night. It was snowing. He stood outside with the snow glittering in his hair and his hands in his pockets. Ara didn't understand gloves.

"Go away," I said. "This is my crying place."

He stood in the falling snow, telling me about why he didn't take pictures anymore, and he looked frighteningly beautiful. I wanted to die with him in the snow, to make love and fall asleep in the snow. Sammi could start clean, then, without us. They both could, she and her baby sister. They would have each other.

I had dreamt of another baby. Two little girls with curls. The second one had brown eyes. Then I dreamt of tomatoes. Canned tomatoes. Stuffed tomatoes. Grilled tomatoes. Sun dried tomatoes sprinkled on a salad of parsley and tiny pistols. When I looked at them in the salad, they were currants, lying there, chaste. But when I picked them up on my fork, they were pistols with a life of their own.

I had been eating tomato soup for breakfast and tomato sandwiches for lunch and canned tomatoes for snacks. I walked to the Armenian grocery store, blocks out of the way, to pick up emergency cans of tomatoes. I dropped off shoes to be repaired by the Armenian shoemaker. I brought them peanut butter cookies. I took Sammi. If I were nice to them, if I stopped trying to forget that I was one of them, the gossip would stop. They would protect me, fellow refugee from the mountains. They would protect Sammi. Ara could like them again.

I crawled inside his coat.

"Sammi needs to start clean," I said. "Without us. Without Turkey. Without Armenia. Just her. Here. We can die in the snow together. It's a perfect night for it. It would be over then. Mama would be over. Sammi would be free."

He pulled away and looked down at me standing ankle deep in the snow trying to get back under his coat. He thought I was drunk, and if I wasn't drunk, I was crazy, and if I was crazy, it was his fault, all of this, us, out in the snow talking about dying. I explained. If his mother was right, if it was my fault, it was easier to kill us, to kill ourselves, than to kill someone else. You couldn't see your own fading light.

He dragged me into the shop. How could I? Could I really do this to Sammi? Other people had done it to us, and now I was doing it for them.

I tried to tell him that it didn't matter who had done it. Someone had always done something to someone. You had to do things to yourself. For yourself. Sammi needed to be free.

"It will be better," I said. "She's only five. She'll forget us."

"Your mother was only five. She didn't forget. You were six."

"I should have, though," I said. "You can't live in the past, you know. I don't want Sammi to live in the past. Or the baby, either. Just think, Sammi would have had a baby sister. Varti will keep Sammi. I'll make her promise. We can write a letter. Aunt Gracia is too old, anyway. It's too much. Even for Mariam. Sean will be a good father. Varti worries all the time, but Sean doesn't. He's a today person. I could shoot us tonight. It would be over."

He wrapped me in his arms. We lay down on the carpet.

"Maybe we should write Sammi a letter first, though," I said. "She might not understand."

Ara kissed me. "Let's talk about it in the morning."

I woke up to a slammed door. Aunt Gracia had delivered Sammi. Ara was helping her out of her snowsuit, chattering to her about photographs being a construct, limited vision, revealing nothing of scent or song, of the shape behind the shadows, the chaos off-camera, the knife behind the back, the child behind the door. A photograph left a hunger for who and why and what happened then. A photograph held attention for seconds, minutes at most. He had learned to hold attention. He had learned how to hold them off, like Scheherazade, spinner of a thousand tales. He who told the best story lived the longest, and living the longest was what it was all about, was it not? He had promised himself that when he got out, he would never tell another story. He wanted to believe that he didn't have to buy his life with his chatter, a life that, in the end, wasn't worth buying.

He had promised himself that if he got out, if he lived, if Sammi and I were real, he would find a way. He would remember why he had gone, and he would find another way. But the truth of prison was the truth. He was a coward.

"Stop it! She doesn't need to know that. What do you know about being a coward, anyway? Sometimes it takes courage just to stay home and do the ironing. Are you crazy? Do you want her to grow up remembering you like that?"

"She's only five," he said. "She'll forget."

"She won't forget. No one ever forgets."

"Can I ask her if she wants a baby sister?" he said.

"You're blackmailing me," I said.

"That's right," he said. "Or I could tell you a story. I tell good stories. People cry. Or laugh. Whatever I decide."

"Don't bother."

"I saved us," he said to Sammi, "with my chatter. Wanna sing?"

I was in a bad mood for the rest of the day. Ara told Sammi not to worry about it. When I got over not getting my own way, I'd be grateful. Two little girls with curls, after all: I wanted those two little girls more than I wanted him.

Ara and Sammi bundled Tiger up and took him for a walk. Sammi loved snow. She thought it was magic. They brought back hot bagels and cold milk.

I refused any warrior names for our daughter. We would name her Gracia, warrior enough.

Aunt Gracia glared at me over the top of Tiger's curls. He was laughing at Sammi. "Leave the past alone," she said.

"It's not the past, it's the present. You're still alive. You're the one who talks about the past. You're getting worse, too."

"I have a right. There are plenty of other names. Janice. Doris. Sandra. Marilyn. Just don't name her for any of those awful singers of yours always moaning about love. Nobody does that. Do you think we moaned about love in the old country?"

Aunt Gracia was talking a lot lately about the old country where courtyards were redolent with perfumed roses and peace, where the coffee was endlessly delicious and the hazelnuts were never bitter, where gossip drifted out of the steam. She wanted to go back.

"To Mariam," I said.

"To everything," she said. "I want to cry for Sam at home."

"This is it, kid," Varti said. "You're going to have to straighten up and fly right. And what are you doing with a pistol in your drawer with that bottle of gin? Mr. Gun and Miss Gin. Just too cute for words."

"Who told you?"

"Aunt Gracia. She was putting some wash back. She's been afraid to say anything to you. She says it's not good for her high blood pressure."

"Tell her to look again. Mr. Gun and Miss Gin have committed suicide. Ara threw them in the river. It's our 'save Sammi' pact. What a waste of gin. I hope it floats to a good home. Bottles can live a long time."

"Talk about positive beginnings," Varti said.

Ara was still having nightmares. Sammi lay rotting on a grassy shore — a five-year-old with flat dead eyes, the flat dead eyes of an empty sunburned sky.

It was summer and the windows were open. Sammi was asleep. We had moved the bed beside the window so the smoke could drift outside. We lay there in the dark, watching the tiny moonglow of Ara's cigarette.

In my dreams, sunlight glinted off the ripples on the wall; the desert silence stirred the leaves. The water wheel turned endlessly, swallowing up the red and the gold light of the maple trees. Sammi was waiting to give her baby sister the third apple. I dreamed of my two girls with curls.

Ara was taking pictures again. He kept his pockets filled with pictures of his three girls so that no matter what happened, he would have us with him.

*fin*